# Anything She Says

Tyra E. Rowell

Abounding Press
Starkville, MS

Abounding Press
Post Office Box 572
Starkville, MS 39760



Book Cover by Stefanie Fontecha

Anything She Says/Tyra E. Rowell.
ISBN 978-1-7321070-1-4

*"A man who loves his wife will listen to anything she says because he believes her love for him is unconditional."*

—Tyra E. Rowell

# Other Books by Tyra

*Unapologetically Being Me*
*Writing through the Valley*

# Dedication

This novel is dedicated to every reader who makes a writer's dream a reality.

*"Kiss me and kiss me again, for your love is sweeter than wine."*
*Song of Solomon 1:2 (NLT)*

# CHAPTER ONE

"Lord, what does a woman have to do to feel good?" Vivian asked in frustration.

Infidelity was not an option for Vivian because of two things. One, it didn't fit her character of being a good, Christian woman. Two, she loved her husband, Jerry, short for Jeremiah. She called him her *Boaz* because she was found as favor in his sight and he didn't pass her by.

She had been sitting in her car for the past 20 minutes frustrated, irritated, and nervous at the same time. It had been 22 days, eight hours, and 45 minutes since Vivian had intimacy with her husband, Jerry. They had been married for three months and had never gone three weeks without sex until now. Even though Vivian refused to take the blame for her sex life being in a drought, she was determined to revive the bedroom. Vivian wanted to feel alive when making love to Jerry, or better yet, when he was making love to her. Feeling alive to her meant being vulnerable and open with him as well as certain body parts exploding when they both climaxed. That was something Jerry lacked to give her in the past three months they have been married. She wanted so badly to enlighten Jerry with techniques on how to get more in tuned with her body, but instead she did the opposite; had no sex at all.

Vivian loved Jerry, but he could be so boring and quick in bed. Always wanting to do the same thing every single time: missionary style. She wondered why the position was called missionary because it didn't give her any room to express her own sensuality. If there were such a thing as bad sex or sex gone badly, this was it. Sex had gone bad. When they first got married, sex was never an issue because they had been withholding sex until marriage. They were in heat from the abstinence so two or three times a day in the missionary position was not an issue. Now Vivian was sore from boredom and faking the feeling. She was beginning to feel like the character, *Celie*, from the movie, *The Color Purple*, when she said the mister just get on top of her and do his business. Those erotic novels she read on a daily basis weren't enough either. She was getting tired of trying the customs of the world to get what she needed. She wanted to try something different and out of the ordinary for her. She made an appointment with a sex therapist to help her, but she was too embarrassed to get out of her car. She did not want to be seen. She wore a wig and dark sunglasses to disguise herself in case she saw a familiar face. If Vivian's mother, Sherri, knew what she was up to, she would be highly upset. She could hear her voice, "Women don't talk about what goes on in their bedroom, Vivian. You leave that to the Lord."

"Oh, well, I might as well get it over with." Vivian sighed. She got out of her car and quickly walked inside the office suite. The last thing she needed was to heed to her mother's words and cancel an opportunity to save her marriage or, better yet, her sex life.

"May I help you, ma'am?" the receptionist asked at the front desk.

"Yes…Um…I'm here to see Dr. Overton." Vivian whispered.

"Ma'am, you have to speak up. I can't hear you."

Vivian looked over her shoulder and spoke a little louder. "I'm here to see Dr. Overton."

"Sign your name here and be seated. You will be called shortly."

Vivian signed her name quickly and sat down. She was so embarrassed and wondered if the people in the waiting area were there for the same reason…sex therapy. Just thinking about the word made her want to get up and leave. As soon as she worked up a nerve to leave, a nurse walked up to her.

"Mrs. Woods?"

"Yes."

"You may come with me." The nurse escorted her through a long hallway which led to another waiting area.

"Just sit here and Dr. Overton will see you shortly. Would you like something to drink?"

"No, thank you." Vivian said quietly.

The nurse started to walk away but turned and faced Vivian.

"I can tell that you are nervous. I want to assure you that no one else knows you are back here. Dr. Overton has a pet peeve about her clients' privacy. She will make sure you are well taken care of. Just relax. You came this far." The nurse left. Vivian inhaled three long breaths to calm her nerves. She was doing something out of her comfort zone and against her mother's values talking to a therapist. Not only was she talking to *a* therapist, but she was also going to talk about her sex life. As soon as she was relaxed, she grabbed a small mirror from her purse and powdered her oily nose. She took off her wig and sunglasses and placed them in her purse along with her mirror and powder compact. She glanced around the waiting room. It was very calm and colorful with peaceful music playing softly. The furniture was comfortable and expensive with beautiful pictures of abstract art on the wall. She was glad to be the only one in the waiting room, because she was finally smiling from excitement.

"Mrs. Woods. How are you?" Dr. Overton asked with her hand extended out for a welcoming handshake from Vivian. She gave Vivian a warm smile as if she was glad to see her. Vivian ascended from her seat and shook Dr. Overton's hand.

"I'm good." Vivian said.

"Well, step into my office." Vivian followed Dr. Overton into her office and a sweet fragrance hit her nostrils and danced with her sensually.

"Wow. Your office smells so good. What is that?"

"It's some candles I bought from *Glen's Fragrances* in Memphis."

"I need to write that down. I love candles."

"I do, too. I hope they are not too strong for you. I can blow them out if they are."

"No, you don't have to do that. I'm fine." Vivian said.

"Have a seat."

"Thank you."

"What brought you here today, Mrs. Woods.?"

Vivian didn't hear Dr. Overton's question because she was too busy checking out her office. She noticed her Master's degree in Marriage & Family Therapy and Doctorate degree in Christian Counseling on the wall. She glanced at the pictures behind her desk on a shelf with a man and two kids. She looked at Dr. Overton's left hand with a three-carat diamond ring. She felt at eased knowing that she was married and had kids. She didn't want to share her intimate thoughts with a single woman.

"Mrs. Woods!" Dr. Overton called her for the third time.

"Yes. I'm sorry. I must have wandered off. I'm a little nervous."

"Please share what's making you nervous." Dr. Overton asked while placing a writing pad on her lap and a pen in her hand.

"I've never done this before. Talking to a therapist is forbidden in my family."

"That may be so, but you came here anyway. Evidently, something has compelled you to seek a therapist. Not just a therapist, but a sex therapist. You do know I specialize in sex therapy, right?"

"Yes." Vivian answered. "I don't care that it is forbidden in my family. I'm feeling like I'm missing something. I'm frustrated. I'm always irritated. I need more from my husband…. I said too much." Vivian said abruptly and jumped from her seat.

"Vivian, please don't leave. May I call you Vivian?"

"Yes."

"Please sit down." Dr. Overton directed Vivian back to her seat. "Let's go over your questionnaire you completed online. As you know the first session is free. Everything we talk about is held strictly confidential. If you speak of endangering yourself or anyone else, I would have to report it. Any questions?"

"No." Vivian said quietly.

"Mrs. Woods. I want you to know I am here to help you not judge you. In order for me to help you, I will need full disclosure from you. You are not the only married woman to come here and you surely won't be the last. So, if you don't mind, let's get started. According to your questionnaire, you've been married for three months."

"Yes. Three months to the love of my life." Vivian smiled.

"You sound happy."

"I am." Vivian said.

"When did you first lose your virginity?"

Vivian coughed. She was caught off guard from the question Dr. Overton asked. Vivian could only respond by saying, "Isn't that personal?"

"Yes, it is." Dr. Overton said nonchalantly. "Vivian, this is a question that was on your questionnaire and you didn't answer it."

"Oh, I must have overlooked it. Sorry." Vivian swallowed hard before responding. "I would have to say when I was in college."

"Ok." Dr. Overton said while looking at the questionnaire. "How old were you?"

"22." Vivian said while clearing her throat.

"I see you missed another question. Have you ever masturbated?" Vivian asked.

"No! That is disgusting. Oh my, Dr. Overton, you are fast tracking this first session. I thought we would at least build a rapport."

"That's what I am trying to do and please understand sex is not something to be ashamed of."

"I'm not ashamed." Vivian said defensively.

"Well, your body language is saying otherwise."

Vivian became silent and exhaled a deep breath.

"Shall we continue?" Dr. Overton said after a few moments of silence.

"I don't know." Vivian said with a disheartened voice.

"Well, let's start over. What brought you here?" Dr. Overton asked with a concerned look on her face. She grabbed a glass bowl from the table near Vivian and asked her, "Would you like some chocolate kisses?"

Vivian grabbed a hand full and begin eating the chocolate as if she hadn't eaten all day. She didn't know how to act in front of Dr. Overton. Sex was something that was never allowed to be spoken of as a child. Her mother didn't talk about sex and she barely saw her mother kiss her father or show any kind of affection. All Vivian heard from her mother about sex was not to do it. It was bad and not for girls. "Good girls don't have sex, Vivian." The voice of her mother was so near to her, she shivered in her seat.

"Are you okay, Mrs. Woods? Would you like a bottle of water?"

"Yes, thank you." Vivian grabbed the water from Dr. Overton and took a long swig of water as if she was dying of thirst. She opened another piece of chocolate and popped it in her mouth.

"So, Mrs. Woods, what brought you here today?"

"Well, apparently I must have sexual issues." Vivian laughed. She always laughed when she was insecure and embarrassed. She took one look at Dr. Overton and immediately stopped laughing. Dr. Overton didn't have that warm smile as before.

"I'm sorry, Dr. Overton. I'm just having a hard time talking about this. Sex isn't easy for me to talk about. It was a forbidden subject in my household when I was a child. As I got older, I engaged in sex, but it still was something I wouldn't talk about in public or to anyone. I know it's not something bad. I know that now. But.... I guess you would say it's a little awkward being here." Vivian rambled, but with a quiet voice, she whispered, "I need help."

"Well, Mrs. Woods, that's why I do what I do. I am here to help you. You have nothing to be ashamed of. I see people from all walks of life in this office. Please know that you are not alone." Dr. Overton sighed before continuing. "What in particular do you wish to accomplish from our sessions? You don't have to give me a list of goals, but if you were to give me one goal, what would that goal be?"

Vivian didn't think past one second. She spoke with no hesitation. "To teach my husband how to please me in bed." Vivian said with a voice so loud and confident that it surprised her to hear it come from her mouth.

# CHAPTER TWO

It had been three months since Junior died and Bianca had already landed prospect number two, Dr. William Holden, a well-known and sought-after neurosurgeon in the state of Mississippi. She had been standing by William's black Mercedes for the past 15 minutes waiting for him to surface from the Lenore Adams Medical Hospital for which he worked for the past ten years. She was so glad to have landed in the arms of a man with money, but she wondered if he was husband material. She had been waiting on this man hand and foot since the day she had met him which was two months ago, because she really wanted the relationship to work. She even vowed to not have sex with William until 90 days according to Steve Harvey's book, *Think Like a Man, Act Like a Lady*, which she had read three times and highlighted with a different color each time. But that didn't help her sustain abstinence. She was on top of William as soon as he said he was looking for a wife which was on their third date. She didn't want to give up the goodies so quick, but she did it anyway against her better judgment. She knew she was grieving over Junior's death when she met William, but she chose not to grieve.

Actually, she was too furious to grieve. Junior was her first love and she *loved* that man. He died of a heart attack sleeping beside his wife. Junior was married to a woman named Yvonne and Bianca didn't know it. The first question she asked Junior on their first date was if he was married. He looked her straight in the eye and then her breast which was on display in a low-cut blouse. He said, "No. I am not married." The second question she asked him was if he was bisexual or homosexual. He said no to both of those questions. It wasn't until his death, she found out that Junior lied to her about being married. They had been dating for three years and Bianca had no clue. The sad part about it was Yvonne invited her to the funeral. She sent Bianca a custom-made invitation with a message written in bold red lipstick, "you didn't know about me, but I knew everything about you." Bianca was so distraught and hurt that she never made it to the funeral. She was scared to confront Yvonne. She just did what she was always taught by her mother, "the quickest way to get past pain is to find comfort in another man."

Here she was trying to land another man, not just to take care of her, but to also marry her. She had just turned 32 two months ago and all she did was dwell on the fact that she was still single with no children. She was thankful for her career, but it could not keep her warm at night. She wanted her own husband and the thought of being with Junior all those years made her angry. She never thought she would be the other woman that the wife knew about. Who would have thought a successful woman like Bianca would be the side chick? Now here she was with another man believing he could be her husband.

Twenty minutes had gone and she was getting impatient waiting on William. Her toes were starting to hurt in her four-inch stilettos William had recently purchased. She wore them just for him because he loved seeing her in stilettos. He told her they made her legs look longer and sexy. That compliment from William made her sacrifice her own feelings and toes just to make him happy.

To ensure she looked just as good as she did when she left home, she glanced at her skinny jeans and red satin blouse which was soaking with sweat from waiting outside for William. She couldn't figure out why William always insisted she wait outside instead of meeting him inside the hospital. She grabbed her iPhone out of her handbag to call him but stopped when she noticed William walking toward her. He gave her a warm smile as he opened the door for her. She wanted to faint due to William's delicious dimples she took noticed to every time he smiled. She smiled back at him and forgot all about her toes hurting. She didn't know whether she was coming or going. Her head was so far in the clouds thinking of that tall, sexy man walking to the passenger's side to let her in the car, that she didn't even make mention of the toddler's booster seat in the back seat when she got in the car. She was intoxicated by his pearly white teeth, cologne, finances, dimples, and him being well endowed. She relaxed in her seat and waited for William to get in the car so she could begin enticing him with her hands instead of conversation.

William was taking a long time to get in the car so she looked for him in the rearview mirror. She saw him talking on his cell phone and said to herself, "Who is he talking to? He needs to get in this car. I've already been waiting for the past 35 minutes. I don't have time for this. I done already cancelled my afternoon appointments just to be with this dude. Now he acts like I'm on his time." As she waited a few more seconds for him to get in the car, she thought about Junior who would never have had her waiting. Junior had a standard of believing that a man should never keep a woman waiting. She couldn't wait on him any longer, but as soon as she touched the door handle, William got in the car. She could tell that he was a little upset, but he turned around and smiled as if her beauty had made his day.

"Bianca, you get more beautiful every time I see you. I hope you are hungry, because I'm famished. Are you ready to eat?" he asked.

"Sure." Bianca said timidly.

"I know this great place for breakfast. It's about an hour from here. I hope you don't mind riding. I promise it will be worth your time when you taste the food. Mm...so delicious. Are you okay?" Dr. Holden smiled.

"Yes, I'm fine. I get a little irritated when I don't eat and I haven't eaten anything this morning."

"Let me see. I think I have some crackers in the glove compartment." he said while brushing against Bianca's leg as he reached for the crackers. When he eased back, he kissed her thigh and all she could do was smile. She didn't want to lose her composure.

"I hope you like animal crackers. I leave some in the car for my son. He loves to eat these things, but only the ones with icing on them." William chuckled.

"Your son? I thought you didn't have any kids."

"Who told you that?"

Bianca looked at him and she wanted to say, "you, dummy", but instead folded her arms and stared at him. She couldn't believe what her ears were hearing. She may have asked him a thousand and one questions when they had first met, but she swore she asked him if he had any children. She didn't know what to think or say because William didn't even respond. He just kept his eyes on the road like he didn't hear a word she just said. She unfolded her arms and opened the small bag of animal crackers. She spoke with a calm voice.

"How old is your son? I bet he's named after you." Bianca asked in a calm and sarcastic voice while crunching on the animal crackers.

"Oh, no. My oldest son is named after me. He's 27 years old." Dr. Holden said proudly.

Bianca almost choked on the crackers. She tried so hard not to laugh so she wouldn't offend the good doctor, but he didn't seem to care that he was putting his huge foot in his mouth.

"Are you alright?" William asked with concern and sweat piercing his forehead.

"I'm sorry." Bianca said while looking perplexed. "Did you say...your oldest son is 27?"

"Yeah, why? What's the problem?"

"How old are you?" Bianca asked with bewilderment.

"I'm 59 years old. I look young, don't I? I will be 60 years young next month! I don't even look like I have a three-year-old?"

"You have a three-year-old! How many children do you have?" Bianca yelled.

"Well, I have eight children."

"Eight!" Bianca yelled even louder. "Oh, H-No!" Bianca wanted to cuss, but she was working on her salvation of getting rid of her spirit of profanity.

She was ready to jump out of the car. She was trying hard to stay calm, but she had never been with a man who was twenty years older than her and had eight kids. She would settle for a man with at least one child and one baby mama with no drama. She wanted to slap the black off of William, but she didn't want to start a fight while he was driving. Today wasn't the day to die. She was afraid to ask him another question, since she had asked him all the right questions in the beginning of their relationship. She needed to know what else he had lied about. As she was processing all that she had heard, she thought of how well-endowed he was in the bed. She figured that explained all the children he had produced and probably with many different women. As much as she didn't want to know anything else from Dr. Holden, she had to ask one more question.

"Are you married?" Bianca asked with her eyes closed and fingers crossed.

"Separated, but it's legal. My wife and I are going through a divorce. Look, I know I lied about a lot of things, but I didn't want to run you off. I can tell by the expressions on your face that you are upset. I really wanted to get to know you and I thought you were a beautiful, sweet, and kind woman that could be a perfect role model for my kids."

"What you mean is you want a nanny!" Bianca yelled sarcastically.

"Bianca, don't be like that. I'm already getting nasty attitudes from my second wife. I don't need it from you, too! Now she's trying to take everything from me!" Dr. Holden said in frustration as he hit the steering wheel with his fist. "My son, my house, even my hard-earned money!"

Jumping out of the car was beginning to sound like a good idea to Bianca, but she wasn't that stupid. She was stupid for believing every word that proceeded out of William's mouth. She was stupid for breaking her vow with God to stop fornicating. She was stupid for thinking William was going to marry her. He was in the middle of a nasty divorce. Now it became clear the reason she couldn't come inside the hospital to wait for him. It became clear why they always ate an hour or two away from their hometown. It became even clearer Bianca needed to get herself some Jesus because Dr. Holden wasn't the one to give her what she needed.

Bianca was still trying to process, *second wife*, that just came out of William's mouth. She was going to try to deal with the fact that he had eight children, but she would be insane to deal with two wives. She was desperate, but not that desperate to put herself in a position to be a nanny *and* a side chick. She didn't know what to say to William, especially when he was beginning to get too distraught. He was swerving on the highway, driving past the speed limit, and cursing at the air. She knew the time was as good as any to say a prayer before jumping out of the car. "Lord, here I am again. I really don't have a legitimate reason for getting myself into various situations which you have to save me time and time again. I don't know why I keep entertaining these strange men, but, Lord, I don't want to die. Please help me! I know I haven't done all I should to do right by you, but Lord, if you would get me out of this car. I promise I will do better. Oh, my God! This man is trying to kill himself! I wonder what this road would feel like if I jump out. Maybe I should wait until he drives past some soft grass. This man is crazy! Why did he have to take me with him? I didn't do anything to him. Lord, I am so scared. I don't know what to do. Please, help me! Tell me what to do to get myself out of this situation. A situation I put myself in because I don't want to wait on You to send me a husband. A husband who is fit just for me. My goodness, this man is going crazy over here. Why does it sound like he is speaking in tongues? Okay, it's time to get out of this car!"

# CHAPTER THREE

Jerry was finally home from a hard day at work and ready to hit the shower. He was a Physical Education teacher and football coach at an urban middle school. He loved his job but at times it could be challenging working with students who thought they were grown and no one could tell them what to do. He was surprised to come home to see Vivian wasn't there. Usually she would be at home waiting on him with supper served and set on the table. He was somewhat relieved she wasn't at home and ran up the stairs to take his shower. He was praying she didn't come home for another hour or so. He wanted to prepare the lesson for the Marriage Ministry at the church. He and Vivian had been leaders over the Marriage Ministry for the past two months. The ministry had grown tremendously since taking it over. The members at church thought they were a lovely couple who were down to earth, approachable, blunt, and transparent. Jerry thought he was unworthy and unqualified to take over the ministry. He didn't know what Pastor Jones saw in him, especially since he was recently married.

Jerry was settled in his home office with a plate of leftovers from the day before that he had warmed up and devoured as if it was his last meal. As he finished eating, he turned on his laptop to get started with the lesson for the marriage ministry. When the laptop was finally loaded to the desktop, a lot of pop-ups flooded the screen. He was disappointed that the pop-ups were there because he thought he enabled the pop-up blocker on his laptop. The last thing he needed was someone to get ahold of his laptop and see pop-ups full of porn on the screen. The volume was loud too. He was glad Vivian wasn't home to hear moans of pleasure coming from his laptop. He turned it off and grabbed his bible to study the lesson. He groaned and sighed, "Lord, help me. I'm trying to do right, but evil is always present." He wiped the sweat off his face. He got up from his chair and walked to the window. Instead of getting on his knees to pray for strength, he peeped out the curtains to see if Vivian had made it home yet. He thought to himself, "This will be the last time. If Vivian was giving me some, I wouldn't have to go this route. A man got needs. I really thought I had this beat. No matter what I do, I can't get it right. Let me get this over with."

Jerry ran to the door of his home office and locked it. He opened his laptop and browsed for his favorite porn videos which were already saved in his *Favorites* file folder. He watched the video and relieved himself sexually. Immediately, he felt worthless of God's grace. He was ashamed because he let God down again.

As he was getting ready to shut down his laptop, a pop-up appeared of a woman who wanted to video chat with Jerry. She was dress provocatively and pleading for Jerry to chat with her. Jerry looked at the woman as if he knew her but wasn't sure. He wanted to find out. As soon as Jerry was about to press yes on the screen to chat, his cell phone vibrated on his desk. It was a number he didn't recognize. He started to ignore it but decided to answer the call. He thought it might be one of his students calling about football.

"Hello." Jerry answered.

"Jeremiah!" Bianca yelled.

"Who is this?"

"Jeremiah, it's me, Bianca."

"Bianca?! What you doing calling my phone? How did you get my number?"

"How do you think, Jeremiah? I didn't think you would still have the same number after all these years but thank God you did." Bianca said.

"What do you want, Bianca?" Jerry asked.

"I need a favor."

"A favor. You're not supposed to be calling my phone."

"Jeremiah, I need your help. I don't know anyone else in this area."

"Please, don't tell me you moved to Southaven."

"No, I live in Olive Branch."

"What do you want, Bianca?" Jerry sighed.

"Can you pick me up?" Bianca asked.

"Pick you up from where? Don't you have a car?"

"Yes, but I'm not in my car."

"Okay, call an *Uber* or a *Lyft*." Jerry shrugged.

"I don't know where I am Jeremiah and I don't want to ride in the car with a stranger. I might get kidnapped or something."

"Jeremiah, are you there?"

Jerry groaned silently. He hadn't seen her in ten years and the last thing he wanted to do was remember the past.

"Yeah, I'm here. Are you near a gas station or store so you can get an address?"

"Yeah, I can see one down the road."

"Alright, text me the address. I'm on my way."

Jerry hit the desk with his fist. He was upset that he didn't get a chance to study the lesson. He read the text from Bianca and he hit the desk with his fist again.

"Dang, Bianca, you got me driving past Como, in the middle of nowhere." Jerry said angrily.

He grabbed his coat and laptop. He figured he would study at the church before bible study if he got back in time. He sent Vivian a text to meet him at the church.

When Jerry arrived at the gas station where Bianca was located, he saw Bianca leaning in the window on the passenger's side of a car talking to someone. He shook his head and blew his horn to let her know he was there. She looked up and waved at him. She gestured to him to wait a minute and continued talking to the passenger in the car. Jerry blew his horn again. Bianca finally walked to his truck.

"You didn't have to blow your horn like that. I was coming." Bianca said.

"You are the one leaning over in that car like you are a hooker or something." Jerry said sarcastically.

"Really, Jeremiah, you don't have to be offensive."

"I'm just saying I have places to be."

"Well, I am not a hooker. Besides, that was one of my friends from college in that car showing off her engagement ring." Bianca said.

"So, where am I taking you? I don't have much time."

"I live on Church Road."

"Dang, Bianca, you're going to have me late for church!" Jerry said angrily.

"Sorry, Jeremiah, but I didn't have anyone else to call."

"Unfortunately." Jerry said.

"Really, Jeremiah. Why you being so mean to me? It's been almost ten years since I've seen you and this is how you act toward me." Bianca said and turned toward the window with her arms folded.

"I don't like being late for church. How did you get all the way out here without your car?" Jerry said.

"I was with someone and he went insane. I told him to let me out of the car or I was going to pepper spray him."

Jerry didn't respond to her statement. He shook his head in disbelief and whispered, "Wow."

Bianca continued to look out the window and said nothing else to Jerry. She was hurt by the things he said. Jerry didn't say anything to her either except to ask her which house belonged to her when he arrived on Church Road. He looked at his watch, said good-bye, and took off.

Jerry arrived at church just in time while the praise team was singing. He looked for Vivian and sat beside her. Vivian gave him a look of concern because he had never been late for church. After the praise team was done, the congregation divided into groups by marriage, single, and children. Vivian and Jerry went to their room to set up for the marriage ministry. While Jerry was setting up the projector, speakers, and his laptop, Vivian mingled among the couples with small talk assuring them that class would begin in a few minutes. When Jerry turned on his laptop, pop-ups flooded his screen. The projector was turned on and the speakers were on blast. Grunting and moaning were all you heard from the speakers. Jerry panicked as he tried to turn everything off, but nothing seemed to work. At that point, Vivian's face was flushed with red speckles. She was not turned on by what she saw, she was mad. She was wondering what was taking Jerry so long to make everything disappear from the screen. She walked over to the podium where Jerry was standing. She unplugged the laptop, unhooked the HDMI cord, and walked out of the room leaving Jerry standing at the podium.

Jerry was embarrassed, but he wasn't going to show it. He simply placed his hands in his pockets and said, "Well, we seem to be having technical difficulties." He laughed. The couples were not. They were staring at him in admonishment. He cleared his throat again.

"I apologize for the technical difficulties. The scripture for tonight's lesson is coming from First Peter, third chapter, and seventh verse. This is the New Living Translation. In the same way, you husbands must give honor to your wives. Treat your wife with understanding as you live together. She may be weaker than you are, but she is your equal partner in God's gift of new life. Treat her as you should, so your prayers will not be hindered."

Jerry realized he wasn't in the right mood to teach the lesson after what had happened with the Power-Point presentation. He apologized again for the technical difficulties and pretended like he was not feeling well. He asked one of the Elders if she could finish the lesson. He gathered his things and left the room. He thought to himself, "It was a good thing Pastor Jones and his wife weren't there to witness this tragedy. I *told* him I wasn't qualified for this."

<u>**CHAPTER FOUR**</u>

Vivian made it home from church and was taking a hot bath while drinking a glass of *Welch's Sparkling Sangria*. She still couldn't believe all those porn sites were on Jerry's laptop popping up all over the screen like a bag of popcorn in a microwave. She didn't know what to think or say about the situation. She knew men watch porn, but not that much. She wondered how Jerry could watch all that porn and not be able to please her in bed. She thought he could have taken some notes. As she continued to sip on her drink, she remembered the looks on the couples' faces at the church. The men had a smirk on their faces as if they were impressed with what they saw, but the women had disgusted looks. And they were trying to cover their husbands' eyes to keep them from watching the screen. The look on Jerry's face was a Kodak moment.

He looked like he had been running a marathon. Beads of sweat were streaming down his cheeks and forehead. Vivian could tell he was embarrassed but didn't care how he felt. She felt like he could have considered her feelings. She wanted to rewind the day and start over from the time she stepped in Dr. Overton's office.

She thought about her visit to a fantasy store. She felt like she was coerced into buying a sexual device. She had never done anything like that before. She convinced herself that it was to be used for the time being until she got Jerry to do what she needed him to do. She stared at it and wondered how to work it. She regretted not asking an employee at the store how to work it. She got frustrated and threw it in the trash. She would rather have the real deal which was Jerry.

Jerry finally made it home from church and he was hoping Vivian wasn't at home to save himself some more embarrassment. He also didn't know what he was going to say to her. He entered the house from the garage and dropped his keys on the table in the foyer. He headed upstairs to get it over with, but when he entered the bedroom he saw Vivian laying on the bed naked reading a book. She was laying on her stomach and her buttocks were the first thing to greet Jerry's eyes. He was astonished and stood there staring at Vivian. He wasn't expecting her to be open to him after the ordeal at the church.

"Hey babe." Vivian said coyly without turning around to face Jerry. She had a feeling he was in the bedroom staring at her, but when she turned around to face him, he was taking off his clothes.

"What are you doing?" Vivian asked.

"What do you think I'm doing? Jerry said while taking off his last piece of clothing which was his boxer underwear.

"You can keep those on." Vivian said. "I'm not in the mood." She climbed out of the bed and put on her nightgown.

"Why you have to tease me, Viv?" Jerry pleaded.

"To show you what you will be missing for a very long time." Vivian said while bending over slowly as if she dropped something on the floor.

Jerry turned sideways and looked at her buttocks on display. He snapped out of it and said, "I've been missing it for the past three weeks."

Vivian walked toward him.

"Vivian, you can't do me like this." Jerry said still pleading.

"Oh, I can do what I want to do."

"Not when you're married." Jerry said.

"How you figure that?" Vivian asked.

"The Bible clearly states that you suppose to give authority of your body to me."

"And what about your body, Jerry?! Do I have authority over yours?" Vivian asked.

"And another thing, have you ever wondered why your wife hasn't been intimate with you in three weeks?"

"And who fault is that?" Jerry asked. "Every time I put my hands on you, you jerked them away. I figured you were tired. You do work long hours at work.

"About those porn sites, Jerry. Why were they all over your laptop? Are you watching that much porn? Am I not enough for you?" Vivian asked.

Jerry sighed and sat down on the bed. "Of course, you are enough for me, Viv."

"It sure doesn't feel that way, Jerry. I feel humiliated ...and...unwanted. How could you do this, Jerry? Is this pleasing in the eyes of the Lord?"

Jerry walked in the bathroom to urinate and didn't respond to Vivian.

"Did you hear my question?" Vivian asked.

"Is what you do in the bathtub pleasing in the eyes of the Lord?" Jerry asked while holding the sexual device Vivian had thrown in the trash.

"I don't know what you're talking about." Vivian said while turning from Jerry.

"Oh, you don't know what I'm talking about." Jerry said mockingly. "I'm talking about you and this." Jerry said.

"That's different." Vivian said and sat on the bed. I haven't even used it. I couldn't figure out how to work it." Vivian said.

"How is this different, Viv? We both are pleasing ourselves and not each other."

"I am not pleasing myself. I was going to but decided not to."

"Why?"

"Because I want you." Vivian said. "And him." Vivian said pointing at Jerry's manly man below.

"Baby, you got us. We standing right here. We can get it on *right now*." Jerry said with confidence.

"I don't want to get it on *right now*."

"Jerry, we need to talk."

"We are talking."

"About our sex life."

"What about it?"

"I'm not happy."

"What do you mean, Vivian?"

"I mean, you don't please me."

"This conversation is over." Jerry said. He walked in the bathroom, slammed the door, and locked it.

"Jerry, don't be upset." Vivian said. "I didn't mean to bruise your ego."

"You didn't." Jerry said. "Here, you might need this."

Jerry opened the bathroom door, tossed the sexual device on their bed, and slammed the door shut. Vivian grunted and yelled, "Once again, I haven't used it yet!" She picked up the sexual device and placed it under Jerry's pillow. She was furious, sexually frustrated, and wanted to annoy him. She turned the lamp light off near the bed, threw the comforter over her head, and cried herself to sleep.

# CHAPTER FIVE

It had been four days since Vivian told Jerry that he didn't please her in bed. They have not said one word to each other. They didn't go to church Sunday either. They just lounged around the house ignoring each other and waiting for the other person to say something. Vivian wanted to ask Jerry why he watched porn, but she didn't open her mouth. She was determined to not be the one to break the ice between them.

Jerry, on the other hand, was elated with joy that Vivian wasn't talking to him. He did miss her morning jokes she told before they went to work. He missed being intimate with her. He was a little dismayed by what she said the other night. He thought about the other women who he had dated, and they had never complained about his sexual abilities. He thought he did good in the area of love making. He felt like he disappointed the one woman he knew loved him unconditionally. When he first met Vivian, he fell in love. It was her smile and the way she carried herself. She had goals and aspirations she wanted to accomplish. She didn't bite her tongue. She said what she felt, but she said it with lovingkindness. Jerry loved that about her. She wasn't afraid to try anything. She always dared him to do silly things. And to hear her now, saying she wasn't happy with their sex life, it pierced his heart.

Vivian decided to see Dr. Overton again and she was not nervous this time. She went to her office without disguising herself. She didn't care if she saw a familiar face. Jerry embarrassed her enough to last a lifetime.

"Hello, Vivian. What brought you here today?" Dr. Overton asked.

"Something happened."

"Tell me about it."

Vivian shared everything with Dr. Overton about the incident at the church and the conversation she had with her husband.

"I've noticed you don't say your husband's name in our session. You refer to him as *my husband*. Is there a reason why?"

"I don't want to say his name. I feel like if I say his name, I would be invading his privacy. He isn't here to speak for himself. Will that be a problem?"

"No. Do what you feel is comfortable." Dr. Overton said.

"Thank you." Vivian said.

"How long has your husband been watching porn, Mrs. Woods?"

"I don't know." Vivian shrugged. "I didn't ask him."

"Do you want to know?" Dr. Overton asked.

"Not really. I just thought it was something men do."

"Not all men watch pornography and it can become an addiction for some. Not all men, but some."

Vivian thought about what Dr. Overton said. She didn't think Jerry would be addicted to porn. She had heard stories from the wives at her job talking about their husbands being addicted to porn, but not Jerry. She thought he was watching it because she wasn't giving him any sex. Now, that her perception had changed, she wanted to know if Jerry was addicted to porn.

"I didn't ask because I thought he was watching it due to us not having sex."

"How long has it been since you had sex with your husband?"

"It will be a month in a few days."

"That's not bad. I have clients who haven't been intimate in a year."

"Oh, no! I couldn't go that long. No ma'am. No way. We might as well get a divorce because I would be thinking if he wasn't getting it from me, then he was getting from someone else." Vivian said.

Dr. Overton smiled.

"Do you love your husband, Vivian?"

"Yes. I love him very much. He's the love of my life. He is my Boaz, a man chosen after God's own heart just for me. He may have his flaws, but he is still perfect for me."

"Vivian, you and your husband really need to have a conversation. Sex should not be a reason for a divorce." Dr. Overton said.

"Divorce! Who said anything about a divorce? I'm not going to leave my husband and he isn't going anywhere either!"

"Good. That's what I want to hear. Lack of communication can lead to divorce. This is not hard, Vivian. If you say you love your husband, love him enough to tell him what you need."

"Wow, blunt, aren't you?"

"Yes I am. I don't take marriage lightly. It is honorable and beautiful. And it is also a *blessing* to have someone who loves you back."

Vivian wanted to say something, but Dr. Overton continued talking.

"God designed sex as well as marriage. Sex is supposed to be enjoyed not obliged. It is a privilege to even have someone to sleep with. Nowadays single folks are succumbing to sexual devices and strange men. Married women are doing the same thing and it doesn't have to be that way."

Vivian sat there and listened to Dr. Overton. She agreed with her, but she wasn't going to let her know that. She didn't want her to know that she was one of those married women who had bought a sexual device.

"I apologize. I said too much." Dr. Overton said.

"No, that's okay. I understand. May I ask a question? What would you suggest a married woman do to tell her husband what she needs? As you know, my husband was furious when I told him."

"There are two types of languages. Verbal and nonverbal. The verbal language did not work with your husband. It's time to try nonverbal. If you can't tell him, then show him.

"But how? He may get mad at that too."

"There's a quote by Woodrow Wyatt, *a man falls in love through his eyes, a woman through her ears*. In the bible, Boaz *saw* Ruth working in the fields. Key

word, he *saw*. You have to give your husband something to see. Be seductive. Grab his hands and put them where you want them. Be creative. Be spontaneous. Wear something different like laced underwear and sweet perfume you think he might like. As a matter of fact, I have a few perfume oils. Here, take this." Dr. Overton said while getting up to grab the sample of perfume oil and handed it to Vivian. "Let him see Vivian. A vivacious and sensual Vivian."
"I will try." Vivian said with a little confidence.

# CHAPTER SIX

Bianca stopped by the gas station to fill her gas tank. While she was waiting for the pump to click off, she thought about the last session with Vivian. She couldn't understand how Vivian could go almost a month without being intimate with her husband. She couldn't last two weeks without being intimate. Actually, she could, but she didn't want to. Sometimes, it was hard for Bianca to understand her married clients because she had never been married. She was in a relationship with Junior for three years, but they weren't living together. If only Vivian knew the real Dr. Overton. A single woman pretending to be married to get more clients for her private practice. She was desperately looking for a husband to love her, and love her only, but she was looking in all the wrong places. If she knew what was best for her, she would stop looking and let the man find her, but she didn't know how to wait for a man. She had never learned or seen from her own mother, Bonnie, what that looked like. Her mother always had a man in her life and a different man for every season. Bianca's father, Julius, was one of them. He met Bonnie at a grocery store when he was looking for a job after his release from the penitentiary. He had served seven years for armed robbery. He and Bonnie hit it off quickly and got married. Nine months later they had Bianca, a spitting image of Julius. She was a daddy's girl and Julius did spoil her more than most fathers. Bonnie couldn't stand it and she made sure she didn't have another child with Julius. She tried her best to keep them apart, but she could not come between them, they were inseparable.

At the age of 14, Bianca's world was shattered. The man she called daddy since she was one had died from an aneurysm. He was sitting in his favorite recliner watching a basketball game. Bianca was never the same after that.

She became rebellious and promiscuous. She wanted to be loved like she did when her father was alive. She had a void in her life that couldn't be filled no matter what Bonnie did for her. Bianca loved Bonnie, but she loved her father more. She believed he understood her more than her mother did. When

Bianca was in high school, she met friends with aspirations and dreams. She sought after her own dreams, but in spite of all the degrees she had attained, it couldn't compensate for being a fatherless child. She quickly realized though that being the only child living with her mother was even harder. She was frequently left alone at home to fend for herself due to her mother's shenanigans with different men even after her father's death. Bianca wanted a different life so school was her focus and God became her father. It was her late grandmother, Beatrice, who taught her how to lean on the Lord for everything. She passed away the same year her father did from breast cancer. When Bianca graduated from high school, she left her hometown.

As Bianca was grabbing the gas pump dispenser from her car, she heard someone from behind her. She turned to replace the dispenser and a woman was standing in front of her with a grin.

"Hi, Bianca." Yvonne said gleefully.

"Do I know you?" Bianca said confused.

"Oh, that's right. I knew about you, but you didn't know about me." Yvonne said and continued with contempt. "I don't know what Junior saw in you, but whatever you did for him, always remember I did it first." Yvonne said.

"You might have done it first, but I did it longer. Bianca said confidently before walking away from Yvonne.

"Wait, don't leave." Yvonne said. "I have something to tell you.

Bianca turned around to face Yvonne. "What more do we need to say to each other, Yvonne? Junior is dead."

"Fortunately, he is." Yvonne said with a smile.

"Excuse me." Bianca said. "Are you saying you're glad he's dead?"

"Child, please, if only you knew what that man put me through! He was dating you while still married to me. And had the audacity to flaunt his infidelity around me as if I wasn't his wife. He didn't hide it and I didn't say anything. I just prayed to my God to send me a way of escape. I was no longer invested in the marriage and neither was Junior. So, I waited." Yvonne said and laughed. "Look at what patience have left me!" Yvonne said while pointing to her brand new white Mercedes. "I have his money, house, life insurance. What do you have?" Yvonne paused and look at Bianca and said, "A heartache."

Yvonne walked away before Bianca could say anything. She didn't want to hear another word from Bianca's mouth. She wanted Bianca to see she was doing great and that she wasn't hurt by her being with her dead husband. Yvonne may have wanted Bianca to think she was not bothered by what she did, but it was all a lie.

Bianca on the other hand, wasn't doing so great. Seeing Yvonne opened a wound of hurt for her because she truly loved Junior. She didn't know what Junior put Yvonne through, but she knew how Junior treated her. He treated her with respect, kindness, and love. She had never known love could feel the way she had felt with Junior. It was not her fault that Junior was not honest with her when they met. She was always told by Bonnie that she was naïve and gullible. She always saw the best in everyone no matter how screwed up they may be.

Bianca held back tears until she got in her car and said to herself, "Bianca, you were not created to be the other woman." As she was about to drive off, Yvonne swerve in front of her car like she was going to hit her. Bianca stopped her car abruptly and she saw Yvonne flipped the bird at her. Bianca calmed herself with slow breaths and put her car in drive. As she was driving off, her phone ranged. She looked at the number and didn't answer. It was a familiar number that she had been avoiding for the past month. It was Bonnie calling her for the umpteenth time. Bianca almost answered the phone, but she decided to ignore the call. She didn't want to talk to her mother. The last time they were together, Bonnie stole her credit card and a couple of hundreds out of her purse. When Bianca confronted her about it, Bonnie lied and got furious with Bianca like she was in the wrong for accusing her. Bianca would have given her mother money if she had asked. It was days like this, Bianca wished her father was alive.

# CHAPTER SEVEN

Vivian was looking forward to going to the movies to be vivacious and sensual with Jerry. Unfortunately, they weren't going to make it to the movies due to being summoned by their Pastor at the church. He wanted to have a meeting with both Vivian and Jerry about the incident that happened at the Marriage Ministry. Vivian tried hard to get Jerry to reschedule the meeting, but he insisted they get the meeting over with. She didn't like it one bit because she didn't cause the incident in the first place. She wasn't the one who got caught with porn on her laptop. She had a mind to pretend to be sick, but Jerry would know she was lying. He always knew when she wasn't honest because she had a tell sign that gave it away. When she was not being honest, she would laugh as if something was funny and she would call Jerry by his birth name, Jeremiah. So, she decided to suck it up and go with him to the meeting because she knew it wouldn't look right for him to go without her. But that didn't stop her from whining on the way to the meeting.

"Jerry, do we have to go to this meeting. I don't want to go." Vivian said pouting.

"Yes, Vivian, for the seventh time, we have to go." Jerry said as he put the car in Park for they had finally made it to the church.

Jerry got out of the vehicle and walked around to the passenger side to open the door for Vivian. Vivian didn't move not one muscle.

"Baby, come on. We are already late. Thank you for taking your loving time getting dressed." Jerry said sarcastically.

Vivian looked at him and rolled her eyes. She said, "Alright. Fine. But I just want to say it doesn't make sense to talk to the Pastor about our problems and we haven't first talked about it ourselves."

"We did talk." Jerry said.

"Oh really? You call what we had a conversation? I don't think so." Vivian said.

"Vivian, I'm not in a mood to argue with you."

"For the record, this is not an argument. We are having a conversation." Vivian said.

Jerry and Vivian entered the Pastor's office. Pastor Jones greeted them with a smile.

"Good evening, Mr. and Mrs. Woods! I am glad to see you both. We missed you Sunday."

Vivian noticed First Lady Jones wasn't in the office. She asked Pastor Jones, "Where's First Lady?"

"Oh, she's in her office. As a matter of fact, she's in there waiting for you."

"Oh, okay." Vivian said and left his office.

"We missed you both this past Sunday." Pastor Jones said while gesturing Jerry to have a seat in the chair in front of his desk.

"We weren't feeling well." Jerry said as he sat down in the chair.

"Jerry, don't take this the wrong way, but is everything okay in the bedroom?"

Jerry was shocked to hear Pastor Jones ask him that. He began to wonder what First Lady was asking Vivian. As soon as he wondered, he felt relieved. He knew Vivian wouldn't tell a soul about their marriage. He believed that and politely said, "With all due respect, Pastor Jones, that's none of your business."

"Apparently it is, when it's displayed all over the projector during the Marriage Ministry."

"Yeah...you see, there was technical difficulties." Jerry said while clearing his throat.

"Jerry, I'm not here to judge you. The Bible clearly instructs us to judge no one. I'm only concerned because I want to see your marriage flourish for many years to come." Pastor Jones said sincerely.

"I want that, too." Jerry said.

Jerry was glad to hear that Pastor Jones wasn't judging him, but he wanted to know the real reason for being in his office. "Pastor, may I ask, why am I here?"

"I have a question for you. Do you think you owe the couples in the Marriage Ministry an explanation for what happened the other night?"

"No." Jerry said with no hesitation.

"Why not?" Pastor Jones asked.

"Because it's none of their business what I do on my personal laptop." Jerry said.

"Put yourself in their shoes, Jerry. If you and Vivian was in bible study for married couples and the speaker had porn on display instead of Bible verses, how would you feel?"

"To be honest, I don't how I would feel because I wasn't in that position."

"Let me put it this way." Pastor Jones said sternly. "Either explain or you will no longer be in charge of the Marriage Ministry."

"Pastor Jones, that's not fair. Vivian and I started this ministry."

"Yes, you did. With my authority to have it here at my church." Pastor Jones said.

"Your church." Jerry mumbled under his breath and chuckled.

"What's so funny?" Pastor Jones asked.

"Look, Pastor Jones, I'm not trying to cause any discord between us. I just want you to understand where I'm coming from man to man. It is not you or your congregation's business what's goes on between me and my wife. How would you feel if someone ask you about you and First Lady's love life? I don't think you would like it one bit." Jerry explained and continued. "The only person who I owe an explanation to is my wife, Vivian."

"You're right, you do owe Vivian an explanation, but you at least owe the married couples an apology for making them feel uncomfortable…. well, the ladies uncomfortable. That's what I want you to understand."

"Alright, I can do that. That was the last thing I wanted to do was to make anyone uncomfortable, especially my wife." Jerry said with concern.

"We will put it on the calendar, two weeks from now." Pastor Jones said with a smile. "And expect me and First Lady to be there."

Jerry wasn't expecting to be ordered to give an apology to a group of married folks who were probably watching as much porn and whatever else in their bedroom. He obliged because he was going to apologize in his own way through the word of God. He didn't know at that time which scripture he was going to use, but he couldn't wait to get home to start searching for the right scripture.

# CHAPTER EIGHT

Going to the movies was the one thing on Vivian's mind as she knocked on First Lady's office door. She heard her tell her to come into the office. She inhaled a deep breath and entered the office.

"Come on in, Mrs. Woods, and have a seat." First Lady Jones said.

Vivian sat down, but she couldn't get pass the fact that First Lady Jones didn't ask her how she was doing or say hi or something. That put Vivian in a not so good mood from the start.

First Lady began reading from the book of First Corinthians, seventh chapter and fourth verse, *the wife does not have authority over her own body but yields it to her husband. In the same way, the husband does not have authority over his own body but yields it to his wife."* She closed the bible on her desk and picked up her coffee cup and took a sip.

"Vivian, have you ever wondered why the scripture started off with the wife first instead of the husband?" First Lady asked while still holding her coffee cup with the inscription, *what a first great lady I am.*

Vivian crossed her legs and replied, "No. I haven't. I was given the revelation that it was an equal task between man and wife."

"It is!" First Lady said excitedly and jumped out of her seat and sat in the chair beside Vivian.

Vivian inhaled another deep breath and exhaled slowly. She was not in a mood for a lecture in regards to her marriage. She surely didn't want to hear it from First Lady Jones who did not know how to talk to women. She had her picks and chooses of who she socialized with. When she talked to some of the women at the church, she didn't make eye contact. She seemed like she was insecure and intimidated by some of the women in the church. She even proclaimed over the pulpit that she wasn't going anywhere. She was well invested in her marriage and no woman was going to come between her and Pastor Jones. Vivian believed some things should be left unsaid instead of allowing your whole congregation assume that your husband is having an affair with someone in the congregation. Vivian thought it was a form of spiritual incest if a Pastor was sleeping with his own flock. She shook her head at First Lady Jones because she almost felt sorry for her. She stared at the heavy makeup on First Lady's face while she was talking. She could see the darkness under her eyes that was concealed with makeup. She could see how tired and stressed she was through the fake smiles she pretended to give on a daily basis.

"Vivian! Did you hear a word I said?"

"I'm sorry, First Lady. I was deep in thought. Please continue."

"Well, as I was saying. The woman is mentioned first in this scripture because we as women hold all the cards in our hands. We know how to pretend to have a headache or not feel well. We get mad and hold it from our husbands. When we do this, we are allowing the enemy to come into our bed and plant a seed into our husband's hearts to either cheat, watch porn, or go to strip clubs.

"Vivian interrupted and asked, "But what if they were doing those things before you met them."

"That still doesn't give wives the right to withhold sex from their husbands! First Lady said with contempt.

"Oh, I'm sorry. Did I offend you? That was not my intention." Vivian said sarcastically in a mild tone of voice.

"No wonder your husband is watching porn."

"Excuse me." Vivian said.

"Oh, I'm sorry. Did I offend you? That was not my intention." First Lady said mockingly and walked back to her seat behind her desk. She could tell she made Vivian upset.

Vivian didn't say anything at that time. She uncrossed her legs and crossed them the other way. She laughed. It was a mechanism of hers, a way to cope when she was upset and didn't want to cry in front of someone. She laughed. First Lady looked at her with contempt and got furious. She slammed her coffee cup down on the desk and coffee spilled on the desk.

"What's so funny?" First Lady asked.

"Nothing." Vivian shrugged.

Vivian could feel tension between her and First Lady Jones. She felt it when she joined the church after marrying Jerry. His church wasn't her choice, but she decided to follow Jerry as he followed Christ. She knew First Lady didn't like it but couldn't figure out the reason. She wasn't going to spend her lifetime trying to figure it out either. Vivian believed if First Lady had something to say to her she will say it. Vivian wasn't the kind of woman to assume anything. She didn't want a relationship with First Lady anyway because she believed she will want to know all her business and she wasn't the type to gossip. She couldn't stand being around women who gossip and talk about other people. She was about to say something to First Lady but heard a knock on the door.

"Come in." First Lady said.

It was Jerry at the door. He asked Vivian if she was ready to go. Vivian said without hesitation, "Yes." She got up from her chair and turned to First Lady.

"It was nice to have a chat with you First Lady. We should get together again." Vivian said.

"That would be nice." First Lady said with her well-known fake smile.

Vivian smiled, but she felt bad for First Lady. She could tell she was unhappy. She prayed for her because she knew how it felt to be that way. She wasn't pleased with how the way the meeting went, but she does have feelings. She wasn't going to allow anyone to talk to her any kind of way. She was relieved Jerry was at the door because she was about to say something she shouldn't. Jerry looked relieved as well. Before she could ask him what his meeting was about, he asked her about the movies.

"Do you still want to go to the movies? It looks like we still have time."

"Sure." Vivian said excitedly.

They arrived at the movies within 15 minutes and exited the vehicle. Vivian was nervous and excited at the same time. She didn't know what to expect, but she was going to try something new.

Jerry had ordered a large popcorn and put tons of butter on it. Vivian couldn't get past the thought of his hands being full of butter. She grabbed lots of napkins.

They had been watching the movie for at least 45 minutes before Vivian took off her jacket and placed it over her thighs. She grabbed Jerry's left hand and placed it on her right thigh under her jacket and kept her eyes on the screen. She could see from her peripheral view that he was shocked. She looked at him with flirting eyes. He looked back at her and grinned.

Jerry leaned over and whispered, "Let's get out of here." Vivian nodded yes.

# CHAPTER NINE

Bianca could hardly get out of bed. She only had two hours of sleep from being scared the night before. She had noticed a black SUV was following her when she left her office late. She didn't take the same route she always took to get home from her office. She drove around a neighborhood twice to be sure it was the same vehicle following her. When she realized it was, she drove to the nearest police department. As soon as she parked in front of the police station, the SUV drove off in haste. Bianca was relieved the SUV drove off, but she couldn't take any chances that the person driving that SUV would be waiting for her to leave. She got out of her car and went inside the precinct and asked an officer for the directions to a restroom. It took her ten minutes to calm down and get herself together before she exited the restroom. She got back in her car and left the precinct. She drove to the nearest *Starbucks,* got her favorite cappuccino, and then drove home. She checked all her windows and doors to make sure they were locked, but the assurance didn't calm her fears. She stayed up that night in her bed with the bedroom door locked, lights on, and a baseball bat in her hands.

Here she was lying in bed with one leg hanging from the side of the bed trying to make it to the bathroom. She finally sat up on the edge of the bed after waiting another five minutes. She got up and ran to her bathroom to keep from urinating on herself. As soon as she exited her bathroom, she heard her cell phone vibrating on her nightstand. She didn't recognize the number and answered, "Hello."

"Good morning, Dr. Overton!" Vivian said.

"Good morning, Vivian." Bianca said with a yawn.

"Sounds like someone had a long night."

"How can I help you?" Bianca asked so she could hurry off the phone.

"I hope you don't mind me calling your cell number, but I had to call to let you know what happened at the movies."

Bianca eyes got wider. "Please do tell."

"Well, I tried something spontaneous. I wore a skirt with no panties, put my jacket over my legs, and I placed his hand on my thigh." Vivian explained.

"Okay and what happened?"

"He responded and I liked it."

"And?"

"And we left the movies."

"Okay, so it sounds like you had a good night."

"Well…"

"Well, what?"

"It didn't end that way."

"What happened?"

"We left the cinema before the movie ended and came back to the house. We ended up in the bedroom. We were all over each other, kissing, and touching. I did something I've never done. I sat on top of the dresser. I was excited and everything."

"But?" Bianca asked.

"I am too embarrassed to say. Within five minutes, my husband was finished." Vivian said.

"Wow." Bianca said quickly.

"That was not the word I used last night."

"Sorry, I didn't mean to make you upset."

"Don't apologize. I'm good. I needed to get this off my chest. I expected him to be relieved before me, since it had been awhile since we've been intimate. I thought he would at least take care of me first. All last night I couldn't stop thinking about some dude I used to date. He knew how to take care of me. This man could really take care of me. I asked myself last night, why my husband couldn't be like him."

"Mrs. Woods, let me stop you right there. You are making a huge mistake comparing your husband to another man. I bet you got a chill down your back thinking about him."

"How did you know?" Vivian asked.

"Been there. Done that. That other man doesn't deserve any thoughts from you. If you and he were meant to be together, you would be together. You are not with him, are you?"

"No."

"Let's focus on what you have and *not* on what you *think* you may not have. Have you been thinking of this other man since the realization of your sex life?

"Not intentionally. Sometimes subconsciously."

"Do you love your husband?"

"What kind of question is that? Of course, I do."

"Do you respect him?"

"Yes. Why are you asking these questions?"

"Promise me, you will never disrespect your husband again by comparing him to another man. He may not know that you are, but he could soon find out. Do you not know the story of Cain and Abel in the bible?"

"Yes, I do."

"Cain killed Abel. Is that what you are trying to do? Kill your marriage?"

"No. Of course, not." Vivian asked.

"Promise me, Vivian."

"Okay."

"No. I want to hear you say it."

"I promise. I'm sorry, I didn't mean to offend you."

"You didn't offend me."

"It sounded like I did."

"I am not offended, Mrs. Woods. I have to make it clear with my clients that I am not the kind of therapist who breaks up marriages. I don't help spouses to destroy what they have by focusing on things they think they don't have from their spouses. I help them to build on what they have because what they have is more valuable than what they don't have."

"I understand." Vivian responded.

"I want you to bring to our next session, a list of things you love about your husband."

"Okay." Vivian said feeling convicted.

"May I ask a question?" Dr. Overton asked.

"Sure."

"Who is the dominant one in the bedroom?"

"That's easy. He is."

"Why not you?"

"What do you mean?"

"Why do you expect your husband to be the dominant one in the bedroom? There's no law stating he has to be the one doing all the love making."

"I don't know. I mean… it has always been that way for me since I've lost my virginity."

"You're not a virgin anymore. You are a wife with a husband. I think your sexual experiences from your past may be causing some conflict in your bed. It's okay for you to be dominant in the bedroom. Besides, you know what it is you like, so take control. Let's talk about this some more at our next session."

"Okay. Thank you, Dr. Overton."

"Mrs. Woods?"

"Yes."

"Please don't call me again on a Sunday morning. It is my only day of rest."

"Sorry. It won't happen again. Have a good day."

"You too."

Vivian felt so bad for comparing Jerry to another man she used to date. She didn't mean to conjure him up, but she was frustrated with Jerry from last night. She was hoping to climax before he did. Afterwards, Jerry took a shower and got in the bed. He didn't talk or cuddle with Vivian. He went straight to sleep like he had a long night. She was so mad at him, she cried.

She had never been in this position before because she always tested the water before committing to having a relationship. She learned the hard way that sex didn't keep a man and it didn't make a man treat her right. She knew the reason for men not treating her right was due to her choosing men who were no good for her. She wanted someone to love and to be loved. She wanted a man to respect her and care about her future as well as her feelings. After her last relationship before Jerry, she decided to not focus on men. She focused on her own life and sought God and all His righteousness. She didn't know when she was going to meet her husband, but she stayed faithful to her God.

When she met Jerry, she wanted to have nothing to do with him because she had got content in being single. Jerry changed her perspective on a lot of things. He treated her like she was his queen and he was her king. There was nothing Vivian could say or do to stop Jerry from falling in love with her. The closer they got, the more he loved her.

As Vivian reminisced on their relationship, she realized Jerry had been good to her, through her flaws and all. And the least she could do was be good to him through his flaws and all. He may not be perfect, but he was imperfectly perfect for her. She couldn't see herself living without him. She got on her knees and prayed to God for repentance. She asked God to give her the courage to not be afraid to give herself fully to Jerry. She asked God to change her perspective toward Jerry. She didn't want to not like him because he couldn't make her happy in bed. She also asked God to deliver him from porn and strengthen their marriage in the name of Jesus. When she finished praying, she put her faith to work.

# CHAPTER TEN

Jerry was in his home office down the hall from the master bedroom. He was avoiding Vivian because he didn't want to have a conversation about what happened after the movies. He could tell Vivian was not happy with him. He thought everything was moving in the right direction until he saw Vivian hopped on top of the dresser. She had never done that before and he was surprised. He welcomed spontaneity, but he liked to keep it simple. He told himself that was the reason for ejaculating early. Vivian didn't keep it simple. She had to add an extra notch to their love-making. He would do it again, but he would rather do it missionary style, if it was up to him.

Jerry cast his thoughts about Vivian to focus on the bible lesson he was preparing for marriage ministry.

He was excited about this particular lesson he was going to give in a few more days. He was supposed to be getting ready for church, but he was still embarrassed after what happened at the last marriage ministry meeting. He wasn't in the mood of faking smiles and pretending other people still liked him. Jerry loved going to his church, but sometimes he felt like the people at his church could be superficial. They acted like they were holier-than-thou but doing all kinds of things as soon as they left the church ground. They sat around and complained about what others did, but not once lifted a finger to help anyone. Jerry believed the scriptures in the Bible about *wolves in sheep clothing as well as people having a form of godliness but denying the power thereof*. Jerry believed there were a lot of wolves working in the ministry department. The ministry department, in his opinion, was being run like a business, not a church. Jerry had been at his church since he gave his life to Christ at the age of 25. He hadn't thought to leave church until he got caught with porn on his laptop. He couldn't understand why Pastor Jones looked at him like he didn't have any skeletons in his own closet. Jerry believed everyone had come short of God's glory. He knew he had shortcomings, but a hypocrite was what he wasn't. When Pastor Jones looked at him with contempt, it gave Jerry a reason to do what he had planned for the next meeting for the Marriage Ministry. He wanted it to be a meeting they would never forget.

Jerry was about to listen to Pastor *John F. Hannah* on his laptop, but he heard Vivian walking toward his office. It sounded like she was dressed for church because he heard her high heels tapping the hardwood floors. He hoped she wasn't dressed for church because he wasn't going to church. Vivian appeared in the doorway of Jerry's office in her red bottom stilettos and red negligee. Jerry pretended as if he didn't see her and acted like he was taking notes. Vivian cleared her throat to get his attention. Jerry looked up from his laptop and smiled. He closed the laptop and said, "Babe, it doesn't look like you're going to church today."

Vivian put her finger over her lips and said, "Shhhh." She walked over to Jerry's desk slowly like she was a model on the runway. She said, "It doesn't look like you're going to church today, either." She sat on Jerry's lap facing him and she grabbed his hand and placed them on her buttocks. Jerry grinned because he realized Vivian didn't have on any panties. He wondered to himself, *"Is this my wife, Vivian?"* He didn't know what had gotten into her, but he didn't want her to stop. He figured this was his chance to make up for last night.

He was about to grab Vivian and place her on the desk, but she stopped him. She told him to not move and Jerry didn't move. She got up from his lap and grabbed his boxers. She pulled them off him gently and sat back on his lap facing him. She pulled off his tank shirt and began kissing him. Jerry moaned. He loved Vivian's kisses. He couldn't get enough of them.

"Do not move. It's my turn." Vivian whispered in Jerry's ear.

Jerry was shocked at Vivian, but he did what she wanted him to do. Just as sure as the sun was shining through the blinds in the window of Jerry's office, it was Vivian's turn. It was intense and hot in that home office. It was a good thing they didn't have neighbors living near them because the neighbors and their pets would have heard them.

# CHAPTER ELEVEN

It had been two weeks since Vivian had surprised Jerry in his office and it had been non-stop with the surprises. Every other day, Vivian was on top of Jerry. Porn and missionary position was the last thing on Jerry's mind. Vivian had dominion in the bedroom and Jerry loved it. He was too scared to admit it because he thought Vivian may be going through a phase. Vivian had him experimenting from all angles. Jerry felt like Vivian had a hold on him because he did whatever she told him to do. There were times, she didn't have to ask. Jerry knew exactly what she wanted when she wanted it.

Vivian always made it a priority to exercise every morning. She made an exception on this morning though. When she woke up, making love to Jerry was on her mind. She woke him up and gave him a passionate kiss. She figured out what got him going was her kisses. She didn't expect to do it again so soon, but Jerry was lying next to her bare naked. He looked so sexy to Vivian and she couldn't stop thinking about how good he made her felt the night before. She decided to make it a round two instead of going to the gym. Jerry didn't mind the extra attention, but he was exhausted. He didn't want to disappoint Vivian so he gave in.

Vivian got out of the bed bare naked flouncing around the bedroom like she was on high. She was twirling, smiling, and shimming. Jerry peeped at her and saw her.

"I see you looking at me." Vivian said.

"Yeah, I am."

Vivian smiled and asked Jerry, "What you have planned today?"

"I might go to the gym." Jerry said. "What about you?"

Jerry watched Vivian grabbed a pair of pretty lace panties with the matching bra.

"When you started wearing panties like that?" Jerry asked.

"Oh, this. I bought this last week. Do you like them?" Vivian asked.

"Yeah." Jerry said.

He liked it, but he also wondered why she was wearing it and who was she wearing it for.

"What you have planned today?"

"I'm going to run errands. Grocery, gas, and maybe a little shopping."

Jerry thought to himself, *In those underwear.*

"Well, I will go with you." Jerry said while getting out of the bed.

"You don't have to." Vivian said quickly. "I got it, babe."

Vivian was going to run errands, but she was going to see Dr. Overton. She had been calling Vivian for the past two weeks asking when she was coming back for another session. Vivian had been ignoring Dr. Overton's calls and voice messages. She figured out on her own with the Lord's help on what to do with Jerry. She didn't want to hear anything Dr. Overton had to say. She told her she would come see her, but couldn't stay long.

"Are you sure?" Jerry asked.

"Yes." Vivian said.

While Vivian was in the shower, Jerry began to get suspicious of Vivian. He couldn't understand why all of a sudden Vivian was changing in their bedroom. It wasn't like he didn't enjoy it, but Vivian wasn't like that when they got married. She was subtle and kept things simple in the bedroom. She never wore a negligee or stilettos. She never wore perfume to bed. She had never ridden on top of him or done oral sex before either. Jerry didn't want to sound alarmed by the new changes, but when he heard Vivian singing in the shower, he had to find out what was making his wife so happy.

He got out of the bed and put on his boxers. He grabbed her phone from the nightstand. He knew her code was his birth year. He looked at her contacts, emails, and phone calls. He saw nothing suspicious. He looked in her purse for her work cell phone. He knew he was wrong for snooping, but he couldn't stop himself. He had to know. He didn't see her phone in her purse, so he looked in the pockets of her coat. Sometimes Vivian put her work phone in her coat pockets. Her phone wasn't in her coat pockets, but he did find a business card and read it, "Dr. Overton, Sex therapist."

When Jerry heard Vivian turn the water off in the shower, he put the card back in Vivian's coat pocket. He dived back in the bed and jerked the covers over his head to pretend like he was sleep. He made it a mission to find Dr. Overton.

Later that afternoon, Vivian finally made it to Dr. Overton's office. She decided to shop before going to see her sex therapist. She wasn't in a hurry, but she was excited to tell her what had been happening for the past two weeks. She checked her emails while waiting for Dr. Overton to summon her. She noticed her email was already uploaded on her phone. She thought it was weird, but she didn't think any more about it. She thought maybe she had checked her email the night before since she did check it religiously.

Dr. Overton summoned Vivian to come inside her office. She was anxious to find out the reason for Vivian missing her sessions.

"What's been going on since the last time we met?" Dr. Overton asked.

"A lot." Vivian said.

"Like what?" Dr. Overton said. She wasn't in the mood to play mind games with Vivian.

"Well, let's just say, I have been released."

"Wow. Are you saying, things worked out with you and your husband?"

"Yes. I don't know where to start. Wait, yes, I do. I prayed and asked God for guidance. I decided to not be afraid to be me anymore. I am a sensual woman and there is nothing wrong with me wanting to enjoy sex with my own husband."

"You're right. There is no shame in being intimate with your own husband. You are married and have every right to enjoy it."

"Exactly! I *want to enjoy* having sex with my husband. I didn't want to admit it at first because I was taught by my mother that sex was nasty. Society teach us to be ashamed. No more. I will not be ashamed or guilty. I am married and marriage is honorable. My bed is undefiled."

When Vivian said her bed was undefiled, she felt uneasy. A few weeks ago, her bed was undefiled with Jerry watching porn and her contemplating to use a sex device. She threw away the sex toy she had bought and she had been praying Jerry get delivered from watching pornography.

"What's the matter? You got quiet." Dr. Overton asked.

"Nothing. I was thinking about my husband. I'm praying he is no longer watching pornography."

As soon as Vivian said that, Jerry walked into Dr. Overton's office. He had been standing by the door eavesdropping on their conversation.

"Jerry!" Vivian said.

"Jeremiah!" Dr. Overton said.

"What are you doing here?" Vivian and Dr. Overton said simultaneously.

"What are you doing here telling all our business to this fraud for?" Jerry said pointing at Dr. Overton.

"Who, Dr. Overton?" Vivian asked.

"She is not a doctor. Bianca doesn't have a doctorate degree."

"Jeremiah, what are you doing?" Bianca asked.

"Don't call my name. You ought to be ashamed of yourself, Bianca." Jerry said. He looked at Vivian, "And you, telling all our business to her."

"Jeremiah, I didn't know you was her husband. She never spoke your name. I didn't even know you were married."

"Vivian, let's go." Jerry said.

"How do you know Dr. Overton?" Vivian asked.

"Let's go, Vivian." Jerry scold.

Vivian stormed out of the office upset. She didn't know how Jerry found out about her seeing Dr. Overton. She wanted to know how Jerry knew Bianca. She had never seen Jerry looked the way he did. He was furious. She couldn't tell if he was furious because she was seeing a sex therapist or the fact that she was telling her business to someone he knew.

Before Jerry left Bianca's office. He asked her, "Does Vivian know about us?"

"No, Jeremiah. I didn't know you were married and she never mentioned your name."

"Good. Let's keep it that way. You are not to see my wife again."

Jerry slammed the door and walked toward Vivian who was standing in the lobby near Bianca's office.

"I don't want you to see her again." Jerry said.

"How do you two know each other?"

"Vivian, this is not the time or place to talk." Jerry said walking away from Vivian.

"Why not? You are the one who followed me here."

Jerry continued walking.

"Jerry!" Vivian yelled.

Vivian said to herself, "What is going on here?"

# CHAPTER TWELVE

Bianca couldn't stop thinking about her last session with Vivian. She didn't have any idea that Vivian was talking about Jeremiah. Even though she was a friend of one his friends on Facebook, she didn't see any pictures of Jeremiah and Vivian. She was surprised to see he had a Facebook page because he was a private person. Bianca didn't browse Facebook like most people anyway. She only made a page to promote her private practice. She was hurt when Jeremiah called her a fraud. She knew she was deceiving people into thinking she was married, but she believed it was the only way to get clients to talk to her. She had never seen Jeremiah so mad and she could tell Vivian hadn't seen him that mad either. Bianca wanted to know why Jeremiah didn't tell Vivian about her. She was sure he had his reasons, but she had never done anything wrong to him. What could make Jeremiah hate her so much? She had some idea why he did, but she didn't want to go back down memory lane. It was unbearable at times and the last thing she wanted to do was get emotional on her date with a man she met at the grocery store. His name was Fabien and he bumped into her basket by accident. Bianca knew she shouldn't be talking to another man, but the chemistry between them was so strong. They exchanged phone numbers and had been talking on the phone ever since they had met. They would talk for hours, even, until the dawn of the next morning.

Bianca thought she had finally landed a good one, but here she was waiting on him at the restaurant where he was treating her for lunch. He was supposed to have been there 15 minutes ago and Bianca was getting concerned. He had never been late for any of their past dates. She called his cell phone and it went straight to voicemail. She thought about leaving, but she enjoyed his company too much. He made her laugh and Bianca believed a man who could make her laugh was a keeper. That was not the only thing she liked about Fabien, even though they just met two weeks ago. Fabien reminded Bianca of Junior. He was kind and gentle like Junior. He had chivalry and showed respect toward Bianca in every way. It could be too early to think of those things about Fabien, but Bianca believed she had a spirit of discernment.

"Sorry, I'm late." Fabien said rushing to Bianca's table. "I'm glad you waited for me. I was praying you didn't get up and leave."

"That's okay." Bianca said. "Is everything okay."

"Yes. Traffic was heavy. There was an accident on the highway."

Bianca thought to herself as she flipped her phone on the table, *you should have called.* Fabien could tell what she was thinking.

"I would have called, but my phone needs to be charged."

Bianca wasn't so sure if she should believe him, but she decided to give him the benefit of the doubt.

"Have you ordered yet?" Fabien asked.

"No. I haven't."

"What's the matter? You look like you have a lot on your mind."

"I'm thinking about that vehicle that was following me two weeks ago."

"Are you still being followed?"

"No. I was thinking about how scared I was."

"You don't have to be scared. I'm here now."

"That's very sweet of you." Bianca said.

The waitress came to their table to take their order. While Fabien was telling the waitress his order,

Bianca thought she saw Yvonne at a table near the front entrance of the restaurant. She gave the waitress her order and told Fabien she would be right back. She got up from the table and walked toward the front entrance to confront Yvonne. By time she made it to the table where she thought she saw her, she was gone. She walked out the front door to see if she was outside. She didn't see her and became confused. She knew she wasn't crazy and hallucinating. She went back inside of the restaurant and returned to her table.

"Is everything okay, Bianca?" Fabien asked.

"I'm okay. I thought I saw someone I knew."

Bianca tried to enjoy the rest of the date the best way she could. Fabien could always get her mind off of things because he had a sense of humor. Within ten minutes she was not looking around the restaurant for Yvonne. As soon she got comfortable and having fun with Fabien. She heard a familiar voice behind her.

"Hello, Bianca. I thought that was you."

Bianca turned around and Yvonne was with a man who could have been her son. She rolled her eyes at Yvonne and turned back around in her seat.

"Who is this?" Fabien asked.

"I'm Yvonne." Yvonne said quickly with her hand out to shake Fabien's hand.

"And this is my date, Alonzo."

"What's up?" Alonzo asked.

"Bianca, you're not going to speak to my date.?"

Bianca didn't respond. She gestured for the waitress.

"May I help you?"

"Yes, we would like our check."

"I hope you're not leaving on my account."

Bianca still didn't respond. She crossed her arms at her chest.

Yvonne got agitated with silence. She bent down beside Bianca and slammed her hand on the table.

"It's rude to not respond when someone is talking to you. Didn't your mother teach you any manners?"

"Did yours?" Bianca asked.

"Ladies, this is not the time or place to act like this." Fabien said.

Yvonne looked at Fabien and said, "You are so right. I am a lady with class. I don't know about this one you're dating. You might want to do a background check on her. She isn't who she claims to be."

"Is there something you need to say to me?" Bianca said when she jumped up from her chair.

"Ladies, people are looking at us." Alonzo said.

"Let them look." Bianca said loudly.

"Baby, let's go. I don't want to be caught on any one's smartphone standing next to this whoremonger." Yvonne said.

"Who are you calling a whoremonger."

"You, darling." Yvonne said while walking away with Alonzo.

"Come on, Bianca, let her go." Fabien said.

Bianca sat in her chair. She was furious and ready to pull Yvonne's lace wig off her head.

"You are too upset to drive. Here, take my keys. I will pay for our food. Go ahead and get in my car. I will be there shortly." Fabien said.

Bianca took Fabien's keys and left the restaurant without looking back.

# CHAPTER THIRTEEN

Jerry had been avoiding Vivian for the past two days since the meeting with Bianca. He also had been avoiding every question Vivian asked about Bianca. He refused to talk about anything concerning a woman he had been trying to forget for the past ten years. He demanded Vivian to stop asking him about Bianca. He knew he owed Vivian an explanation, but he wanted to talk about it when he was good and ready. Not when Vivian wanted to talk about it. He had finally finished the lesson he was preparing for the Marriage Ministry and was super excited that he needed a release. He wanted to tease Vivian, but there was tension between them. He didn't want to go back to watching porn either. He had been praying for deliverance and didn't want to break his vow to God or himself. He shut down his laptop. He no longer had Kleenex and lubricant in his office because he got rid of it. He believed in getting rid of things that could tempt him to sin. He got on his knees and prayed for strength to resist his urges.

When he was done praying, he went to the bedroom. He saw Vivian in her purple robe which was open showing her black panties and no bra. She was ironing her clothes getting ready for church. He had contemplated on whether he should bother her and his urges won. No matter how tensed things were between him and Vivian, he loved her to the core. He knew she had been crying about the way he had been treating her these past two days. He wanted to show that he cared about her feelings. He took a shower and came out of the bathroom with a towel wrapped around his waist.

Vivian saw Jerry looking at her and pretended like she didn't care he was in the room. She continued to iron her clothes and watched the news on the television. She was still mad at Jerry for having the audacity to demand her to stop asking questions about Bianca. A woman who was no longer Dr. Overton. She was a woman by whom Vivian felt threatened. She had made up in her mind that she was not going to be intimate with Jerry until he talked to her. When Jerry came out of the bathroom with his chest exposed and glistening, she almost fainted with weakness. Vivian had a weakness for Jerry's body which was masculine and ripped. She felt weak, but she continued to stand strong.

Jerry could tell Vivian was falling weak when he walked out of the bathroom. He knew Vivian had a fetish for his chest. She was always grabbing his chest and back when they made love. When he saw her look at him, he flinched his muscles in his chest. One way or another, Jerry was determined to make love to the woman he loved.

Vivian saw those muscles flinched in Jerry's chest and wanted to faint in his arms. She knew what Jerry was up to and decided to tease him as well. She turned off the iron and took off her robe. She sat on the bed and began putting lotion on her body starting from her neck to her legs. Even though her back was turned to Jerry, she could tell he was watching her.

"Jerry, do you mind putting lotion on my back?"

Jerry quickly obliged while grinning. He felt like a king knowing he was winning his queen over to him. He got in the bed behind her and grabbed the lotion from Vivian. He rubbed the lotion on her back slowly and gently. He worked all the way up to her shoulders and started to massage them. Vivian enjoyed every stroke from his hands and said, "That feels so good." Jerry grinned to himself and so did Vivian. As good as it felt to feel Jerry's hands on her shoulders and his hard manhood on her back, Vivian still stood her ground about not giving in to him. She stood up from the bed while Jerry was still massaging her shoulders and said, "Thanks, babe."

Jerry was still sitting there on his knees in the bed shocked and ready with his hands in the mid-air. Vivian felt like a queen breaking her king down. It felt good to Vivian knowing she had such power over him. While she was looking for a bra in the top drawer of her dresser, Jerry got behind her. She could feel his breath on her neck and he smelled so good to her. She felt Jerry's left hand on her thigh and she knew then if he went anywhere near her vulva, it was over. Her will to stand strong was going to come tumbling down.

Jerry knew what he was doing. He may not have known what got Vivian in the mood a few weeks ago, but he knew now. He knew where Vivian loved to be touched. When he heard Vivian moan with pleasure, he knew she was going to give in to him.

Vivian could no longer stand her ground. She did resist a little, but not enough. Vivian loved Jerry and she couldn't resist him any longer. He was the love of her life, and she believed God sent Jerry to her. She wasn't going to allow any woman to come between her and her man.

# CHAPTER FOURTEEN

Marriage Ministry was packed full of folks. It was so packed, they had to move to a larger room. There were folks at the meeting who had never been to one meeting since the beginning. Jerry wasn't expecting the meeting to be that jammed and packed. He thought it would at least be the same couples who were present at the last meeting when he was caught with pornography on his laptop. At first, he was anxious to teach the lesson he spent two weeks preparing. Now he was getting nervous and wondered whether he should go forward with the lesson he had prepared. He glanced at Vivian who was sitting to his far right. He realized how supportive Vivian had been to him. He didn't know what he would do without her being by his side. She was truly his helpmate and she was the one who encouraged him to step out on faith with the Marriage Ministry. He looked around the room. Instead of seeing the couples through his spiritual eyes, he saw a room full of nosy people. He knew they were there to hear what he had to say so they could have something to gossip about. Pastor Jones and his wife were sitting on the front row smiling and whispering to each other. The room was quiet, but the stares from the couples were talking loudly. Jerry felt somewhat small and it brought him back to his childhood. A time when he saw his dad beating a man in the street for not having his money. He was only ten years old and the thought of hurting another human being was far from his mind. He was a young boy watching Spiderman and spending his time riding his bike with his friends until it was dark. He had never seen so much blood splashed as his dad punched the man in his face with his fist. Jerry remembered the look on his dad's face when he asked him to join him in beating the man. While standing there numb and confused, he urinated on himself. Jerry's dad called him a punk and a sissy. He was not going to be a punk on this day.

Jerry decided to go ahead and teach what he had prepared for the couples. He began the lesson with prayer and requested the couples to find Romans, third chapter, and 23rd verse in their Bibles or Bible app. He talked about how God's people fall short. He had a PowerPoint presentation with pictures of biblical men and women who fell short. He had a picture of David and Bathsheba. A picture of Rahab who had changed her life. A picture of Moses and his rod. A picture of Noah being drunk. The couples were nodding their heads in agreement.

Jerry went on to say, "I have come short of the glory of God, too. Some of you were at the last meeting and saw what happened on the projector. If you weren't here, I'm sure you heard about it. I am not pleased with the way my wife and I are being treated as if we have leprosy. When we came to church Sunday, we saw you all whispering and looking at us. No one came to us and spoke to us like they used to do. It's ashamed how we as Christians shun folks when they fall. The Bible says in Galatians, the sixth chapter, that if someone is caught in sin, you who live by the Spirit should restore that person gently. But you must be careful or you will fall into the same temptation yourself. Ladies and gentlemen, I want to show you what that looks like."

Jerry went back to his PowerPoint presentation and began showing pictures of some of the couples. The first picture he showed was Pastor Jones' armor bearer, Joe, at the strip club. He showed First Lady at a fantasy store with a basket on her arm buying sex toys. He quickly showed pictures of some of the men flirting and touching young women who were members of the church. He showed pictures of some of the wives at a male strip club with their dollar bills. The last, but not least, picture Jerry showed was an *Instagram* post captioned, *our son, Aaron Jones the third* with Pastor Jones and another woman who used to be a member of the church. At this point, the members were flabbergasted at the audacity of Jerry showing pictures of their private lives. Some of the men were standing on their feet yelling at Jerry to stop showing pictures. Jerry yelled louder, "John, eight, seven, he that is without sin, cast the first stone. You can't and neither can I." Two of the ladies walked out of the meeting. Pastor Jones was at the podium where Jerry was standing trying to calm everyone down in the meeting. First Lady was looking ashamed and wanted to leave the meeting immediately, but she thought it wouldn't look right for her to leave. She was all about image. Vivian was sitting in her seat shaking her head at Jerry. She felt like what Jerry did was unnecessary and unbelievable. She couldn't believe Jerry sunk this low and she realized she didn't know her husband as she thought she did.

"Okay, everybody, let's quiet down." Pastor Jones said calmly.

"Pastor, I'm not done" Jerry said.

"Oh, yes, you are." Pastor Jones said sternly.

Jerry looked at Vivian and she turned her head. She was disappointed in Jerry and couldn't look at him.

"Everyone, sit down please." Pastor Jones said and looked at Jerry who was still standing at the podium, "You, too."

Jerry was hesitant to move, but when Pastor Jones gave him a look like this wasn't the day to mess with him, Jerry obliged. He sat down beside Vivian feeling defeated because he didn't finish his lesson. He still had more to say. He wanted the couples to know those pictures weren't shown to condemn or judge them. He was not a judgmental person and he wanted them to know that. He wanted them to know no one in the room could judge anyone. At first it was about flipping the script on the couples, especially Pastor Jones. Jerry didn't like the way he was insinuating that there was trouble in his and Vivian's sex life. There may have been, but Jerry wasn't going to talk to him about their private life or anything else. Jerry felt bad things didn't turn out the way he thought.

"As bad as things look right now, Mr. Woods made a good point. We all have fell short of the glory of God, including me. I know the last picture is... well, it is me. My wife, Carla, come here, baby."

Pastor Jones summoned her to join him by the podium. She stood by him and held his hands.

Pastor Jones continued, "My wife and I worked through this. She knew all about it."

One of the men in the congregation interrupted him, "Well, we didn't know." He grabbed his wife's hand and they both left the meeting. Three more couples got up and left. Pastor Jones dropped his head in shame.

"Just like Mr. Woods said, if anyone is without sin, cast the first stone. I am not without sin. I have done my wrongdoing and I have also asked the Lord for forgiveness. Since we are in Christ Jesus, we are no longer condemned by something we have done in the past." First Lady declared.

First Lady Jones looked at her husband, "Baby, is there anything else you want to say?"

Pastor Jones shook his head no and left the room. His armor bearer, Joe, got up and said, "I think it will be best if we adjourn this meeting... until further notice." He left the room with First Lady Jones.

The remaining couples looked at Jerry and he got up to gather his lesson and materials. He and Vivian left the meeting in silence.

# CHAPTER FIFTEEN

Bianca was still ignoring Bonnie's phone calls. She was not in the mood of arguing with her mother and answering her questions about why she was ignoring her. Even though Bonnie knew the reason for Bianca ignoring her calls, she would still act like she didn't do anything to her. Bonnie loved to make Bianca feel like she was the reason for her problems. Bianca refused to allow her to dictate her day and make her feel worthless. She had another date with Fabien. They were at the movie cinema to see the movie, *Black Panther*. Then, afterward they were going to Red Lobster to eat and talk about the movie. Bianca was a Marvel fan and her favorite character as a child was Incredible Hulk. She was looking forward to Fabien's company and her mother would have to wait another day to talk to her. That's if she decides to answer her phone call which was going to be no time soon. Bianca loved her mother, but their relationship was strained. It didn't matter that she had a degree in counseling, she couldn't restore their relationship. She could not fix her mother and herself at the same time. It took two people to work at a relationship and lately Bianca felt like she was alone in trying to fix her and Bonnie's relationship. She was exhausted and needed a break from the dysfunction.

Fabien had been the highlight of her life because he treated her different than any other man. He didn't treat her better than Junior did, but he was close. He sent her white lilies to her office and she was surprised that he knew she loved white lilies. She was almost smitten by him. After her ordeal with Dr. Holden, she wasn't going to let her guard down. Her tower was going to stand tall and wide as long as she needed it. She was tired of being duped by men who had no intention of giving her what she needed the most. That was to be loved unconditionally.

As her and Fabien were waiting in line for popcorn, she looked around the cinema. She thought she saw a familiar face in the crowd. She whispered, "That looks like Dr. William Holden." He was walking inside the cinema with a young woman on his arm. Bianca thought to herself, *she is probably a nanny*. She prayed he didn't see her standing in line because she didn't want to entertain that foolishness. She turned around and faced the long line of people ahead of her and Fabien. Three minutes later, she heard her name being called. She pretended like she didn't hear William calling her and started talking to Fabien.

"Hey, Bianca." William said while tapping on Bianca's shoulder.

Bianca ignored the tap on her shoulder. Fabien motioned her to turn around.

"I thought that was you." William said.

"Hey, Dr. Holden. What brought you to this part of town." Bianca said with an irritated look on her face.

"We are here to see the movie like everybody else."

Fabien cleared his throat to get their attention.

"Fabien, this is Dr. Holden and Dr. Holden, this is Fabien." She looked at William's date. "And what's your name, sugar? Isn't it past your bedtime?"

"Well, we better get in line before we miss the movie. It was nice seeing you again, Bianca." William said as he was walking off with his date.

"It sure wasn't nice to see you." Bianca mumbled.

"He seems nice."

"Key word, seems. Just because it looks like a duck doesn't mean it quacks like a duck." Bianca mumbled.

"What you say, baby?"

"Oh, nothing. I'm just excited about the movie."

"Me too." Fabien said.

Bianca was relieved Fabien didn't ask about William. She didn't want to explain how she knew him because she wanted to forget she had ever met him. She believed some things needed to stay in the past and William was one of those things. He was a mistake to learn from and nothing more. Junior was also a mistake, but she loved him too much to clarify him as someone she regretted knowing. If she had found out Junior was married while he was still alive, she believed she would have continued to see him. She was glad she didn't have the chance to choose between right and wrong. She would hope to have made the right decision.

Bianca wondered when she would get over Junior because she didn't want his memories to jeopardize her dream of having her own husband. A husband who was compatible and allowed her to be herself. A husband who didn't lie and cheat. She was tired of crying over a man who lied to her for three years. He was never going to marry her or give her children. He was never going to give her a house like he promised. She was never going to meet his family who he claimed lived in Georgia. He was already doing those things with Yvonne, a woman who he was married to for twelve years. A woman who Bianca didn't know about, but Yvonne knew about her.

As Bianca thought about Junior and his lies, she grabbed Fabien's arm. They were sitting in the theater waiting for the previews to show before the movie. She looked at Fabien and wondered if he could be the one to make her dream come true. She was tired of dating the same kind of dudes who meant her no good. She was tired of picking those dudes. She knew if she wanted something different, she had to try a different method to get what she wanted. She vowed to not have sex with another man until she was married. Her grandmother, Beatrice, told her before she died to seek the Lord and all His righteousness and all those things would be added to her. Bianca was having amnesia like she didn't remember all the things Beatrice taught her about life and men. She was acting like she had no upbringing in the Lord and she knew the Lord well. She used to talk to God every day when she was a child. After Julius died, she talked to God when she needed Him to get her out of something she caused upon herself.

When the movie ended, Bianca and Fabien went to Red Lobster. They stayed for almost two hours talking about the movie. Bianca had a good time with Fabien and didn't want the date to end.

"I had a good time tonight." Bianca said while walking to the car with Fabien.

"I did, too." Fabien said.

"I really don't want this date to end." Bianca said leaning on Fabien.

"It doesn't have to. Guess what I'm thinking."

"What?"

"I'm thinking about seeing your office where you work."

"Okay."

Bianca and Fabien arrived at her office.

"Here, it is." Bianca said.

"It's nice and comfortable."

"That's the key to make my clients feel safe and comfortable."

"Well, it's working."

"Can you excuse me, Fabien? I have to go to the restroom."

"Sure."

Bianca put her coat and purse on the desk and went down the hall to the restroom. Fabien watched her and waited to hear the sound of doors close down the hall. He grabbed her purse and found her keys. She had three keys on the keyring. He made copies of them and placed them back in the purse. He sat down on the couch in a hurry before Bianca came back in the office.

# CHAPTER SIXTEEN

Sleeping in her bed alone was not what Vivian had in mind when she married Jerry. She refused to be like her parents, Sherrie and Victor, married to each other, but sleeping like roommates. The night her and Jerry came home from Marriage Ministry, they had a heated argument. It was their first argument since they have been married and things hadn't gotten better. Jerry continued to not answer Vivian's questions about Bianca. She couldn't understand how he refused to talk about a woman who was suddenly threatening their marriage. She did not like being put in a position to assume anything that may be going on between Bianca and Jerry. She wanted to know the truth and since Jerry wouldn't tell her anything. She decided to get answers from Bianca. She didn't care about Jerry demanded her to not see her again. He couldn't tell her what to do just like Vivian couldn't make him talk to her. She knew Jerry hated confrontation, but the issues at hand was provoking her to be selfish. Not only did Jerry become silent about Bianca, he had the audacity to demand her to not ask him another question about Bianca. What he did at the Marriage Ministry didn't make him look any better. He was getting worse by the minute. She wanted to call her mother and talk to her about it, but she decided not to tell her anything. She didn't want to give her mother a reason to dislike Jerry. No matter how bad things looked, she still believed Jerry was a good man.

It had been a week since Vivian and Jerry had been intimate. She wanted to sneaked into his office where he was sleeping on the sofa, but she was still mad at him. Vivian was going to hold a grudge for as long as she could until Jerry understood what he did was wrong. She wondered if Jerry was in his office watching pornography. If he was, she prayed he get delivered. She also prayed there was nothing between Jerry and Bianca. If it was, she didn't know if she could take the heartache. Vivian learned about praying for her husband from her grandmother, Mimi, who was a God-fearing and sensual woman. Mimi didn't bite her tongue when it came to talking about the Lord and being intimate. She told Vivian that being intimate is more than having sex. She also told Vivian to never hold intimacy from her husband because the Bible says so. Vivian could hear her voice as clear as day as if she was in the room with her. She hadn't heed to Mimi's or God's voice. She had everything on lockdown from communication to intimacy with Jerry.

It was almost time for Vivian to get up to get ready for work and she groaned at the thought of getting out in the rain. It was 5:58 a.m. and her phone rang.

"Who is calling at this time of morning? It better not be a teacher calling because I told them to not call me until 6:30 in the morning. Oh, wait, it's my personal phone." Vivian said to herself.

"Hey, Mimi." Vivian said when she answered the phone.

"Hey, baby."

"Is everything okay, Mimi?"

"Yes, all is well with me. I called to ask you that question. Is everything okay?"

Vivian hesitated to answer and then said nothing.

"Well, I take your silence as a no. I was in my prayer closet this morning and the Lord laid you on my heart."

"God is always sending a ram in the bush." Vivian chuckled and cried quietly at the same time.

"How's Jerry?" Mimi asked.

"I guess he's doing alright."

"What do you mean, you guess? Don't you both live together?"

"Yes, of course, Mimi. I didn't mean it like that."

"Vivian, I'm sensing that there is something going on with you. If it's a problem with you and Jerry. You already know what to do. Have you been praying lately? You need to keep the lines open with the Lord, baby. He will not give you more than you can bear. Marriage isn't easy, but it is worth fighting for, especially when you know it was ordained by God. Do you believe God put you two together?"

"Yes, I do." Vivian said wiping away her quiet tears.

"Well, baby. Fight on your knees, not with your emotions. Feelings can't be in a spiritual warfare. The devil doesn't fight fair and neither should you when it comes to your marriage. Let nothing come between who God has joined together. That even include yourself. Sometimes, us, women, can make things worse by doing what we want to do. It takes two to make a marriage work."

"What if you are fighting to make it work alone?"

"Baby, you're not alone. God is with you. Have you not been reading your word? Yea, though I walk through the valley of the shadow of death, I will fear no evil, for thou are with me!" Mimi declared. "And remember, it is just a shadow."

"Thank you, Mimi."

"For what, baby."

"For checking on me."

"Always, baby. I believe everything is going to be alright. Jesus is on the main line, just tell him what you need."

"I will." Vivian said.

"I mean now."

"Right now?"

"Yes. The devil waits for no one. He is always on the lookout for someone to devour. You have to stay on the lookout, too. Staying alert and watchful, always praying. Even when you don't know what to pray, pray anyway." Mimi declared.

"Father God, in the name of Jesus, I declare my marriage to be victorious! I may not know what is going on with my husband, but God, you know. There is nothing too hard for you, God. You are able to fix what is broken. So, I'm declaring right now, God, that my husband is delivered from pornography. I declare my husband is faithful to me. I declare my husband is still the man I married. I pray he continues to be before your face, Lord, always seeking you and your righteousness. Lord, I pray you give me the wisdom and guidance on how to handle things in my marriage. For I don't know everything, but you do, Lord. I pray you give me the strength to get through this valley,

Lord. It may not be as big as I think it is. In Jesus name, I pray, Amen."

"Amen. Do you feel better?" Mimi said.

"Yes, I do."

"So, Jerry is into porn, huh?"

"Mimi!" Vivian laughed.

"Well, I will say this. You can only do that for so long. After a while, you're going to want the real thing. Ask me how I know."

"Mimi, no."

"Child, you don't know me." Mimi laughed.

"I don't even want to know." Vivian said.

"Well, baby, I got to go. My husband over here being frisky."

"Okay, Mimi. I don't need to know all that."

"Baby, there's no shame over here. We love to get frisky. You, young folks aren't the only ones having fun."

"Okay, Mimi. I will talk to you later." Vivian said.

"Have a good day, baby. Love you."

"Love you, too."

Vivian thought about what Mimi said about having fun. She laughed and said to herself, "I hope I still be doing it when I get her age."

# CHAPTER SEVENTEEN

Jerry was in the kitchen making breakfast on a work day. He made her favorite foods which was grits, eggs, turkey bacon, and toast. He was hoping his peace offering would break the tension between them. Vivian was giving him the silent treatment and he couldn't stand it. He missed her laughter, kisses, touch, and conversations. For the past week, it was work, come home, take a shower, and get back on the sofa to sleep and start over. He was sorrowful for some of things he said to Vivian the last time they had talked. He didn't mean to hurt her feelings by telling her it would be better to live on the rooftop than to be in the house with a nagging woman. He felt bad for telling her to think what she wanted to think about what may be going on between him and Bianca. He didn't want her to think he was being unfaithful be-cause that was far from the truth. He didn't know what else to say to get Vivian to stop asking about a woman he had been trying to forget for the past ten years. He believed the past is something to not dwell on, so why talk about it. He didn't want to entertain the thoughts of all the things Vivian may have told Bianca about their marriage. He was still upset about that but decided to let it go for the sake of having his wife back.

His phone rang and he stared at the phone. Pastor Jones' name was on the screen. Jerry declined the phone call. He had been avoiding his calls and dodging people at work who were members at his church. Jerry hated confrontation and he had no idea why he had problems with people confronting him. Confron-tation made him feel intimidated by the other person, especially when they bombard him with questions he wasn't ready to answer. He needed to reflect on what he was going to say to them. He thought he would be able to tell Vivian anything, but the story behind Bianca made him paralyze. He refused to talk about her at the moment. He needed more time and ex-pected Vivian to respect his wishes.

Jerry entered their bedroom with a plate of food and a glass of orange juice. Vivian was rushing out of the bedroom combing her hair. She didn't acknowledge Jerry standing in the room. He set the plate and glass on the dresser. He waited for Vivian to acknowledge his presence, but she didn't say one word and neither did she look at him.

Jerry cleared his throat and said, "Good morning."

"Good morning." Vivian said without looking at him.

"I made you some breakfast this morning."

Vivian looked at him and said, "Thanks, but I don't have time to eat."

Jerry was disappointed but understanding. He was disappointed in himself for putting Vivian in a situation to be cold to him. He didn't like the cold look she was giving him. Jerry didn't see that glow in her eyes she used to give him when they got married.

"Baby, can you stop for a minute. I have something to say."

Vivian continued to put on her clothes for work.

"I'm sorry." Jerry said.

"Sorry for what?" Vivian asked.

"For the things I said to you. I didn't mean it."

"Oh, yeah, you did mean it. It came out of your mouth. What does the bible say about what defiles a man? It's not what goes into a man's mouth that defiles him, it's what comes out of his mouth."

"So, you want to use the word on me this morning. Alright, what does the bible say about a woman submitting to her husband for he is the head of the wife."

"And what am I? The tail?" Vivian asked.

"That is not what I said."

"Then, what are you saying?"

"Vivian, I didn't come in here to argue."

"I'm not arguing with you. I simply asked a question, but this is what you do. Run, when people ask you a question about something you did." Vivian said.

Jerry stood there quietly.

Vivian continued, "You fail to realize that I'm here because I want to be. I can be with any other man, but I'm here with you, Jerry. And another thing, talking to you is not nagging. I have no idea why you wish to not talk about Bianca, but I want you to know it's not right to have me in the dark. I do not need the extra anxiety."

"Vivian, I have one question. If you are here because you want to be here, then why am I on the sofa?"

Vivian wanted to scream at Jerry. She exhaled and said, "You're right. Why are you on the sofa?"

"Because you put me there."

"No. I remember you walking out of the bedroom with your pillow after your nagging comment."

"I did?"

"Yes, you did."

"Well, I want to come back."

"Ok." Vivian said and continued getting prepared for work. She grabbed her purse and coat to leave.

"Can I get a kiss?" Jerry asked.

Vivian wanted to tell him no, but she thought about something Mimi told her. *Baby, no matter how mad you may be at your man, still give him a kiss. But let him know you are still mad at him.*

Vivian kissed him on the lips and said, "I'm still mad at you. We are not done talking."

Jerry tried to get more than a kiss.

"What are you doing? No, honey, you're not getting that kind of kiss... for a long time."

"Come on, babe. You know I love to kiss."

"Don't you need to go to work?"

"I'm already dressed."

Vivian walked out of the house and left to go to work. Jerry was taking his time leaving because he had an itch to watch a little bit of porn before he went to work. He paced the floor in the bedroom. He walked to his office and then back to the bedroom. He wanted to give in to his urges, but he remembered his vow to God to not watch porn again. He went to the kitchen and ate the breakfast he had cooked for Vivian. He looked at his watch and saw he still had about 30 minutes before he had to leave for work. He turned the television on to watch the news. He watched it for about ten minutes and he started to get antsy. He looked at his cell phone on the table and checked the time. He had about 10 more minutes until he had to leave for work. He was trying everything else to avoid his temptation, but he didn't try prayer. He believed he could stop watching porn cold turkey. He also believed he wasn't addicted to it. He remembered telling his co-worker, Thomas, that there was no such thing as being addicted to pornography. Thomas tried to tell him it wasn't easy because he had the same problem. Jerry didn't want to hear that nonsense. He believed if he wanted to stop, he could.

Jerry looked at his cell phone again and said, "Lord, forgive me." He grabbed his phone and went to his office. He typed in the porn address. As he was waiting for the page to upload, he grabbed the tissue. When he looked at his phone, a security blocker was on the page. He typed in the address for the website again. The security blocker appeared on the screen.

"Vivian!" Jerry yelled.

Jerry realized Vivian had put a blocker for porn sites on their Wi-Fi. He was disappointed at first, but he was relieved. He knew God had given him a way of escape from pornography. He thought to himself, "I can't be tempted, if I don't have access to it."

# CHAPTER EIGHTEEN

Fabien was at Bianca's door to take her on another date. They had been seeing each other more since the incident with Yvonne at the restaurant. Bianca opened the door and surprised Fabien with a passionate kiss on his lips. She had been wanting to do that since they had met in the grocery store and she was glad he kissed her back. Fabien had been a gentleman toward Bianca, not making one intimate move toward her. Bianca liked that about him and was grateful to have a guy friend who wasn't trying to have sex with her. He made her feel safe and comfortable to be herself around him. She could not get enough of his sense of humor. Fabien was taking her to a restaurant in Cordova which was an hour drive from Olive Branch. He was paying for everything because he wanted to pamper her. Bianca prayed she didn't see

Yvonne. She decided to call the police on her for stalking if she did see her in Cordova. Bianca loved going to Cordova to shop, eat, and laugh at the *Laugh Out More Comedy Club*. Bianca was excited about going to see one of her favorite comedians, *Lavell Crawford*.

Bianca had an awesome time with Fabien and she felt like the date was ending too soon. Fabien walked her to the door and told her good night.

"Do you want to come in?" Bianca asked as Fabien was walking back to his car.

"Sure." Fabien said.

When they entered the apartment, Bianca screamed, "Oh, no!"

"Stay right here. Let me check the house."

Bianca was too shocked to move. She couldn't believe the house she had bought last year was vandalized.

"There's no one here. I'm going to call the police." Fabien said.

Bianca finally took small steps to the living room which had glass all over the floor from the pictures that were hanging on the wall and the lamps from the end tables. She picked up a picture of her and Junior which was near the fireplace. It was taken out of the frame and Junior's face had been blackened out with a marker. Her face was torn from the picture. Bianca threw the picture back on the floor and continued to view the rest of the damages. The cushions on the couch in the living room were torn apart. Her desktop on her desk in her guest room which was an office was cracked. Every book from her bookshelves were thrown on the floor. She went to her bedroom and turned on the light. The first thing she noticed was the word, 'whoremonger', written on her wall above the headboard of her bed. It was written in red. She climbed on the bed and smeared the written word and sniffed her finger. It smelled like lipstick. The comforter and sheets were on the floor. Her clothes were hanging out of the dresser and chest. Some clothes in her closet were not on the hanger. They had been thrown on the floor. Bianca was livid in disbelief at the audacity of someone to come in her house and vandalized it for no reason. She had not done anything to anyone to deserve such an act.

Fabien joined her in the bedroom and told her the police were on the way. When the police arrived, an officer took her statement. One officer took Fabien's statement while another officer took pictures of the vandalism. Bianca had never seen so many officers in her house.

"Do you know who could have done this?" the officer asked Bianca.

Bianca wanted to say something sarcastic, but responded, "No. I don't have a clue who could have done this."

The officer continued asking odd questions which had nothing to do with the vandalism. Bianca was getting agitated with the officer. She asked if she could answer questions another time. She was not in the mood to be on good behavior responding to silly questions. There was no telling what she may let slip out of her mouth. Then, she would be arrested and spend a night in jail.

She waited outside on the front porch with Fabien for the officers to finish their report. When they left, Bianca and Fabien entered the house carefully to not step on glass. Fabien grabbed a broom from the kitchen to sweep the glass off the floor. Bianca asked to be excused to take a shower. She felt drained and a hot shower always made her feel better. She put on some comfortable clothes and went back in the living room. She noticed Fabien had cleaned as much as he could clean off the floor. The room was still a mess, but at least it didn't look the way it did before. He was sitting on the couch waiting for her return. Bianca sat next to him.

"Thank you for a lovely evening. I had fun."

"So, did I? Lavell cracked me up."

Bianca laughed, "He was so funny. I'm glad we got a chance to take a picture with him. Do you have your copy?"

She was feeling down about her house, but suddenly Fabien made it less noticeable. He always knew what to say to her to make her feel better. She grabbed his hand and laid her head on his shoulder. She didn't know what she would have done if she had come to the house alone. She didn't have any friends in Olive Branch to call and she most definitely couldn't call Jeremiah.

"Do you mind staying the night? I mean, you can sleep on the couch. I don't want to be alone."

"Sure. No problem."

"Thank you. I really appreciate this."

Bianca brought Fabien cover and pillows to sleep on the couch. She was glad to have him at the house. She went to bed and tried to go to sleep. Sleep wouldn't come because Bianca was busy brainstorming who could have vandalized her house. She first thought of Jeremiah, but what reason would he vandalize her house. Then she thought of Dr. Holden, the insane one, who wanted to kill himself after learning his wife was taking all his money. She quickly dispersed that idea. He didn't know where she lived and was glad she didn't have the chance to invite him to her house.

"Who could have done this?" Bianca asked herself.

She looked at the ceiling and glanced at the red writing on the wall behind her head.

"Whoremonger. What a nasty word to call some-one." Then an idea came to her mind, it made her sit up in her bed.

"Yvonne! But how?!" Bianca said to herself.

# CHAPTER NINETEEN

When Bianca got up the next morning to make coffee, she walked pass the living room and noticed Fabien was not on the couch. The sheets she had given him were neatly folded on the couch along with the pillows. She called his name and there was no answer. She looked in the bathroom and the guest room. There was no Fabien. She ran outside to see if his car was still in the driveway, and it was not there. She wondered why he had left without saying anything to her. She went back in the house thinking maybe he had left a note. She searched the living room for a note between the cushions on the couch, under the couch, and near the end tables. There was no note from Fabien. She plopped down on the couch in disappointment thinking how strange it was for a man who made her feel so safe to leave before she had awakened. She barely slept last night. She had dreams of Yvonne stalking her at her private practice demanding to know why she took Junior from her. She slept on and off and didn't know how she didn't hear Fabien leave. She had no idea what time he left either.

She quickly got up from the couch and ran to her room to get her house phone. She dialed Fabien's phone number and heard the operator say, "You have reached a number that has been disconnected or is no longer in service." Bianca didn't hang up the phone and that's when she heard the operator say, "Good-bye." She dialed Fabien's number again thinking she must have dialed the wrong number. She grabbed her cell phone and looked through her contact for his name. She clicked on his name to make the call. She heard the operator say, "You have reached a number that has been…" She hung up the phone on the operator in disbelief. As she sat on her bed with the phone still in her hand, it vibrated. She answered an unknown call, "Hello."

"There was no answer.

"Hello."

Still no answer. She hung up the phone and threw it lightly on her bed. The phone vibrated again. She answered the unknown call again, "Hello."

There was no answer, but she could hear someone breathing.

"Hello. I can hear you breathing."

Still no answer. She disconnected the call again but held the phone in her hand.

"What if something had happened to him? What if he stole money out of my purse?" Bianca said to herself. She grabbed her purse and found her wallet. Every card was in its place and she counted her cash. It was the same amount she had placed in there the day before.

"Ugh, I'm going crazy in here."

Her phone vibrated again. She glanced at the number on the screen and didn't recognize it. She answered it with hope.

"Fabien?"

"No, this is Vivian."

"Vivian?" Bianca asked in confusion.

"Yes, Mrs. Woods."

"Oh, yes. I'm sorry. I was expecting someone else."

"I'm sorry to call you this early in the morning. I hope I didn't wake you."

"No. I was awake. How can I help you?"

"I know Jerry told me to not see you again." Vivian said.

"Excuse me. I'm sorry. Who is Jerry?"

"Jerry. My Jerry. My husband, Jerry."

"Yes, that's right. Jeremiah." Bianca said.

"Are you okay, Dr. Overton?"

"Yes, I am. I have a lot on my mind. Continue, please."

"As I was saying, I know Jeremiah told you not to see me again. I need to talk to you. Can you meet me for coffee this evening?"

"I don't think that is a good idea, Mrs. Woods. The last time I saw your husband, he was furious."

"That is true. That's why we are going to meet somewhere he won't see us."

"We can talk on the phone."

"No. I want to see you in person, Dr. Overton. Please, it is important."

Bianca sighed. She was not in the mood to entertain Vivian, especially after feeling she was being duped once again.

"I don't know, Mrs. Woods."

"Please, Dr. Overton. I promise he won't know we are talking."

Bianca wanted to tell her no, but she needed a distraction from her own problems.

"Okay. Text me the address."

"Thank you! Is 5:00 a good time?"

"Sure. I will see you then."

Bianca disconnected the call quickly.

"What the blank does she want?" Bianca said to herself. She needed coffee. She went to the kitchen to make her coffee, her phone rang, and the word unknown displayed on her screen again.

"I don't who this is playing on my phone, but you need to stop calling me or I will call the police!"

"Bianca, this is your mother!"

"Oh, my bad, I thought it was someone else."

"Is everything okay?" Bonnie asked with concern.

"I'm fine, Mama." Bianca said while making coffee. "Why are you calling me with an unknown number?"

"Because you have been ignoring my calls."

"I've been busy."

"Too busy to talk to your mother?"

Bianca did not want to talk to Bonnie, not at a time like this. She wanted to hang up on her and act like it was a bad disconnection. She had other things on her mind than to be arguing with a thief who she called Mama. Her mother had not been the same since Julius died and her ways have destroyed their relationship. Bianca desired to be close to her mother, but Bonnie made it impossible.

"Mama, was there a reason you called?"

"Yes, I did. I know you are still upset about me borrowing money from you without asking."

"Borrowing? Mama, you stole a credit card from my wallet." Bianca yelled.

"Girl, you better watch your voice. I am still your mother!" Bonnie said.

"I apologize, Mama." Bianca sighed.

"Now, look, I know our relationship is not great and sometimes I can be difficult. I want us to be close. You and Julius were close. I want that."

Bianca didn't respond. She had heard this talk from Bonnie many times. She wasn't believing a word out of her mouth.

"Did you hear me, baby?"

"Yes, I heard you. Can we talk about this later? There's someone at my door."

"Are you going to call me back?" Bonnie asked.

"Sure. Okay, bye."

Bianca laughed. "Sure, mom. I will call you back at an unknown number."

The doorbell rang again.

"Coming." Bianca said.

She made it to the door and a delivery man was standing at the door with white lilies. She was shocked to have received such beautiful flowers. She signed for the flowers and closed the door. She looked for a card on the flowers.

Bianca read the card aloud, "I'm sorry."

# CHAPTER TWENTY

Vivian parked in front of a small coffee shop named, *Coffee Anytime,* to meet Bianca. She decided to meet her there because she knew Jerry wouldn't dare step his foot into the place. When they were dating, he told her he would rather make his own coffee than spend that much money on a cup of coffee. She was glad Bianca agreed to meet her because she was tired of waiting for Jerry to answer her questions. She entered the coffee shop and looked for Bianca. She was sitting to the far right in a corner like she didn't want to be seen. Vivian went to the checkout line to order herself a coffee and then she joined Bianca at her table. She noticed Bianca looked like she had been crying. Vivian was concerned and also contemplating whether she should ask her what was wrong. Their relationship was already on shaky grounds. She still had no idea who Bianca was to Jerry. For all she knew, she could be an ex-girlfriend. She felt that Bianca may not want to confide in her. The Jesus in her saw she needed a word and she couldn't ignore the signs.

Bianca was sitting in a corner sipping on her coffee and when she saw Vivian walk through the door, she wished she had never agreed to see Vivian. She liked Vivian, but she was in a vulnerable state of mind. She didn't want Vivian to see her that way. She needed Vivian to see the warrior in her who had her life together. The longer she sat there in the tranquility of the coffee shop, the more her mind traced through the incidents with her house and Fabien. She tried hard to not think of Fabien, but he was constantly invading her thoughts. The way he smelled, laughed, and treated Bianca made her fall in love with him. She knew she shouldn't have fallen for him after knowing him for only a few weeks, but it was hard not to. He had her on cloud nine and she felt stupid for allowing it. She rubbed her cold hands together to warm them up and that's when she noticed her fake wedding ring was not on her left hand. She had a flashback to the day when Jerry called her a fraud. She thought to herself, *I may be a liar, but I am not a fraud.*

"Hey, Dr. Overton. How are you?"

"Please call me Bianca and I'm good. How are you?"

"Good."

There was silence. They both sipped their coffee. Bianca broke the silence.

"So, what did you want to talk about?"

"Before I get into that. May I ask is everything okay? You look... exhausted?"

"I am. I had a long night."

Bianca thought she had said too much. She didn't want to form a friendship with Vivian when she was supposed to be her client.

"Do you want to talk about it?"

As tempting as it was for Bianca to talk because she really needed a friend. She declined.

"I rather not." Bianca said.

"Okay. I know I may not be a good candidate to confide in, but I want you to know God got you. He would not put more on you than you can bear. You may not believe it, but you are in my prayers."

Bianca cleared her throat to keep from crying and said, "Thank you. So, what did you want to talk to me about?"

"My husband, Jerry, how do you know him?"

"I think you should ask Jeremiah."

"I did and he won't say, so, I'm asking you."

"It's so strange to me why Jeremiah haven't told you about me."

"Why is it strange?" Vivian asked.

"Look, Vivian, the only reason I'm talking to you now is because I like you. I like your strength, the way you carry yourself. I wish I could be more like you, strong, happy, and confident."

"Dr. Overton, I mean Bianca, you are stronger than you think. You have a lot going for yourself. You have a degree, your own practice, taking care of yourself, and married." Vivian looked at her hands and saw there was no wedding ring. Bianca put her hands under the table.

"Bianca, I'm so sorry. I pray things work out between you and your husband."

Bianca was about to tell Vivian the truth about her not being married, but her phone vibrated on the table. She answered when she saw the number from her private practice displayed on the screen. She answered it.

"Hello."

There was no answer. She could hear breathing.

"Hello."

Bianca disconnected the call and dialed her secretary, Margie's cell phone number.

"Hello." Margie said.

"Hey, Margie, are you at the office?"

"No. I left about 30 minutes ago." Margie said.

"Someone just called me from my office."

"Well, it wasn't me, and plus I locked up the place. There was no one in the building when I left. Is everything okay?"

"I will call you back." Bianca said quickly and disconnected the call.

Vivian was listening and watching Bianca panicked in front of her.

"Is everything okay?" Vivian asked.

"I have to go." Bianca said.

"Wait, do you need anything?"

"No, I got it." Bianca said.

"Okay, I pray all is well. Wait, before you leave, how do you know Jerry?" Vivian asked.

Bianca was in a hurry to get to her office and she looked at Vivian. She could tell Vivian was anxiously afraid to know.

"He's my brother." Bianca said as she swiftly left their table.

Bianca wanted to stay and explain more to Vivian, but she had to leave. She was hysterical and wanted to know who was calling from her office. She knew she was crazy for going to her office alone and not calling the police. She didn't want to involve the police after how they made her feel in her home. She sped through the traffic on the highway. When she got about ten minutes out from the coffee shop, traffic slowed down. There was an accident ahead of her on the highway and she was furious. She looked around at the traffic trying to figure out a way to detour. She signaled and moved to the far-right lane on the highway. As she was moving slowly in the right lane, she saw a familiar face. He was standing on the corner of a fast food restaurant with a sign saying, *need money for food and gas*.

"That looks like Fabien." Bianca whispered.

# CHAPTER TWENTY-ONE

Jerry was exhausted and ready to leave work after a long day with teaching P.E. and coaching football. He wanted to get home, eat, shower, and go to bed. He hoped Vivian was at home cooking him a full course meal. He was tired of eating takeout food. He started to send a text to Vivian requesting a meal but decided against it. He didn't want to make her upset because he was hoping to make love to his wife.

As he was walking to his truck, he noticed some cars were parked near it. At first, he was startled, but as he got closer to his truck, he recognized the owners of the cars. A few men from the church got out of their cars when Jerry got to his truck. He was not in the mood to talk to anyone, especially folks from church. Joe, the armor bearer was the first one to approach him.

"Mr. Woods, we need to talk."

Jerry sighed and put his belongings in the truck and closed the door. He put his back to the door and crossed his arms.

"Okay." Jerry said.

"We want you to know what you did was foul." Joe said.

"Okay." Jerry said.

"Man, some of the men's marriages aren't the same." Joe said while pointing at the other three men who were standing near him.

"That's not my fault." Jerry said nonchalant.

One of the men stepped up to Jerry and Joe held his arm out to block the man from getting in Jerry's face. It didn't stop the man from yelling, "It is your fault, man, with your arrogant self, standing there like you didn't do anything wrong!"

Thomas, who was Jerry's assistant football coach and best friend, was walking to his car when he heard the man yelling and stepping up to Jerry. He walked faster to assist Jerry.

"What's going on here, Jerry? Are you alright?"

"Yeah, I'm good." Jerry said still standing with his back to the door of his truck with his arms crossed. He didn't flinch or make a move when that man stepped up to him.

"It's okay. Let it go." Joe told the other man.

"It's a bunch of bull, man." The other man said while shoving Joe's arm away and he walked back to his car.

Thomas continued, "Jerry, do you need me to call the police?"

Joe intercepted, "That is not necessary. Right, Jerry?"

"No. We're good, Thomas. You can leave." Jerry said as he walked over to where Thomas was standing.

"Are you sure, man? These folks look like they want to give you a beat down." Thomas said.

"I'm sure, man." Jerry said and gave him a fist bump before he left.

The other man said aloud so Thomas could hear, "You don't belong here, this is a church matter anyway."

Jerry walked back to his truck and stood in his same spot as before. He looked at Joe for him to speak because he didn't need to say anything.

"So, as I was saying before, we feel like what you did was foul, Mr. Woods. We don't think we deserved having our business displayed for the world to know. To be honest, it was not your place to tell our business." Joe said.

Jerry didn't respond. He stood there like he was processing what Joe was saying.

Joe continued, "What did we do to you to be treated like this? Our wives won't talk to us and what you did to Pastor Jones was even worse. Pastor Jones is in a troubled state of mind."

"Joe, it is not my fault his marriage is in trouble. He shouldn't have done what he did in the first place. He should have been faithful."

The other man yelled, "Faithful?! What about you?"

"What about me?" Jerry asked.

Joe replied, "You haven't been faithful either, Mr. Woods."

"I have never cheated on Vivian."

"Not in the same sense as we have, but you have not been faithful."

"How you figure that?" Jerry asked defensively.

"Watching porn is not being faithful." Joe said before the other man could respond. He was trying to keep the conversation peaceful but it didn't stop the man from yelling, "And jerking off," while Joe was talking to Jerry.

"What he meant to say is you are pleasing yourself without Vivian. If what you are doing is honorable, then why not include your wife, Vivian when you are watching those videos?"

"I don't have to stand here and listen to this. I'm going home" Jerry said.

The other man said, "See, I told you this would be a waste of time."

Jerry got in his truck and drove off. He left the men standing in the parking lot confused and frustrated. He didn't care how those men felt or about what they had to say. He was upset that they had the nerve to accuse him of being unfaithful to Vivian by watching porn and not only that, but also pleasing himself alone without her.

"How dare them? How do they know if I don't include Vivian? They can't assume that I'm pleasuring myself without her."

Jerry heard himself out loud and said, "Well, I am, but you don't know that! You have no right to know my business."

Jerry sighed and said, "Lord, I didn't have any rights to know their business, either. I feel bad, but I don't regret telling it. The people needed to know."

Jerry continued talking to God, "I had to let them know they had no right to point their fingers at me. I am not the only one with sexual issues."

Jerry was so caught up in stating his facts but wasn't taking the time to stop talking and listen to what God had to say about the situation. He looked at himself in his rearview mirror and checked to make sure his nose was clean. He was being proud and showing no remorse for his part in the situation. He was too busy looking at what others were doing, but not looking at himself. He was acting like the man described in the Book of James in the Bible as a hearer of the word and not a doer. He was like a man who looked at himself in the mirror, walked away, and immediately forgot what manner of man he was.

Jerry picked up his phone and browsed his contacts to call his dad, Richard. He was not his biological father, but he was honored to call him, dad. Richard practically raised Jerry as his own ever since he was eight years old. It took him two years to win Jerry over, but he never gave up on Jerry. He was determined to be who Jerry needed him to be and that was his dad. It didn't matter to him that Jerry was not his biological son because blood didn't make him a dad. It was his actions that made him kin and Richard made sure to show Jerry how much he loved him and that he was his dad no matter what.

"Hello." Richard said.

"Hey, dad."

"Hey, son. What are you up to?"

"Nothing. I decided to call you and see how you were doing?"

"I'm good."

"Are you on the tractor? I can hear it stalling."

"Yeah." Richard said.

"You and your toys. Dad, you don't have a garden."

"Hold on, now, this isn't no toy. I don't need a garden to drive my tractor." Richard chuckled. "Talking about toy, you wouldn't last five minutes on this thing."

"You don't have to worry about that because I'm not getting on it." Jerry said.

There was silence on the phone.

"How's Vivian doing?"

"Good. She's good."

"I'm asking, how are you and Vivian doing?"

"Oh, we good, Pops, no worry here."

"Son, you know I know you. When something is bothering you, you don't talk much. On any other day, you would be talking my ear off."

"That's not true."

"Okay, if you say so." Richard said.

Richard continued, "I know marriage isn't easy, but it can be. We only make it hard for ourselves by thinking and making choices like we don't have a spouse. When two people get married, it becomes a partnership. You have to think and make choices for the both of you. Keep Jesus in the middle. You got to keep Jesus in the middle. God got the outside like a fence around you both, but Jesus in between you both makes everything run smooth."

Jerry listened to his dad talk about marriage for ten more minutes. He thought of his late mother, Evelyn, who died from breast cancer six months before he married Vivian. Ever since he could remember, he never saw Richard raise his voice or a hand at his mother. They were always kissing, hugging, and cuddling. As a boy, he thought it was nasty, but when he became a man, he understood. He dreamed of one day being just like his dad, Richard. He wanted to be with a woman who loved him as much as he loved her. He prayed for that woman and he went through many trial and errors before he got the right one; Vivian. Jerry thought about Vivian and he felt convicted because he knew he was being selfish. He wasn't putting his ego aside to be the man she needed him to be. He didn't want to fail as a husband.

"Do you hear what I'm saying, Jerry?"

"Yeah, dad, I hear you. Communication is the key."

"If you want her legs to continue to open, you got to keep the lines open. You got me?"

"Yeah, dad. I got you."

"Alright, I got to get off this phone. It's about to get dark out here."

"Okay, dad, I'll talk to you later."

"Love you." Richard said.

"Love you, too."

# CHAPTER TWENTY-TWO

Bianca wasn't one hundred percent sure if that was Fabien on the corner begging for money, but she was about to find out. She turned into the parking lot of the fast food restaurant. She cracked her window on the passenger side. It was a good thing the windows on her car were tinted.

"Hey!" Bianca said while waving a twenty-dollar bill out of the crack of the window.

He walked over to the car smiling and when he made it to the car to grab the money, Bianca let the window further down to expose her face.

"Fabien! I thought that was you." Bianca said.

Fabien grabbed the money and ran away from Bianca's car.

"Oh, no, he didn't take my money."

Bianca put the car in drive and chased Fabien around the parking lot of the fast food restaurant. When she got around to the back of the restaurant, there was no Fabien. Bianca yelled from the driver's window.

"Fabien! I know you are out here! Why are you hiding?! You, son of a …"

Bianca stopped herself before the vulgar language came fleeing from her lips. She parked her car and sat there with tears flowing from her eyes. She was so disappointed. Not in Fabien, but in herself. She was lonely and tired of the wrong men approaching her. She didn't go out there looking for these men, but she did choose to entertain them. She couldn't figure out why. She knew she wanted to be loved, but why was it so important to her to be loved by a man when she needed to love herself first and more.

"Oh, my God, help me! I can't keep doing this to myself. I deserve better than this! What is wrong with me?!" Bianca cried. "My daddy didn't raise me to be this weak."

Bianca heard in her spirit, "And neither did I."

"God, it's been so long since I've heard you. I need to do better and I will. You're right, God. You didn't raise me to be weak for I am strong. I am a royal priesthood, a peculiar person, and I am one of the chosen. I was made in your image. I shall live and not die. Yes, Lord, I am more than a conqueror. I will make it through this! I will not grieve, for the joy of the Lord is my strength."

Bianca didn't care who heard her. She was in a communion with her God and no one, not even Fabien, was going to get in the way of that. She was hurting, but she still had hope. She found some tissue in her purse and dried her eyes. She exhaled, "Everything is going to be alright."

As soon as she put the car in reverse, she saw Fabien run past her. He was running fast and he was like Lot in the Bible, didn't look back. Bianca watched him run across the street.

"Fabien, I pray you get what you need and not what you deserve for hurting me. I speak deliverance in your life. May God lift you out of darkness and place your feet on a path of righteousness. I don't know what you may have going on with your life, and I don't care to know, but may Jesus reign in your dreams every time you close your eyes. I pray you see redemption. I pray your eyes open to God's glory for you really do need it. I pray you don't hurt another woman like you did me, for no one deserves to be deceived. You had no intention on loving me, but that's okay. God loves me and I know that is good enough. I pray this prayer in Jesus name. Amen."

Bianca hadn't forgot how to pray nor how to get in God's presence when she needed Him. Her grandmother, Beatrice, taught her well. She taught her no matter how bad or good things get in her life, always pray. Always get before the Lord and let praise forever be on her lips. Bianca was three years old when Beatrice taught her to pray because Beatrice believed she was never too young to know the Lord. Bianca didn't know how to choose good men, but she knew how to pray.

She drove off the parking lot and continued driving to her office. She hadn't forgotten about the phone call received earlier when she was with Vivian. She was getting nervous because she didn't know what to expect.

She parked her car in front of the building and got her pepper spray out of the glove compartment. She got out of the car and put her cell phone in her back pocket. She hurried to the front door and unlocked it. She went inside of the building and locked it. She turned on every light switch she could find. She refused to walk down a dark hallway. She made it to her office and opened the door. She was appalled by what her eyes were seeing. Her mouth flew open. Then, the tears welled up in her eyes again. She couldn't utter the words. All she could do was walk through her office which was vandalized. She couldn't believe how quickly her life was spiraling out of control.

"I need a drink." Bianca said as she plopped on the sofa which had not been touched. "And I don't even drink."

Bianca laid on the sofa and closed her eyes.

"This is a dream. This is a dream, right?"

She opened her eyes and looked around her office.

"Nope, it's not a dream." Bianca said as she laid her head back down on the sofa and closed her eyes.

"This is ridiculous!" Bianca screamed as she stood up.

"Look at this mess! What have I done to deserve this?!"

Bianca walked around her office through the clutter of books and paintings she had on the wall. She checked her file cabinets and they were still locked. She was relieved because that was where she kept her clients' notes of their sessions. She looked inside the desk drawers to make sure nothing was stolen. She reached in the back of one of the desk drawers and found what she was looking for. A stack of pictures she had printed of her and Junior. She threw them in the trash and said, "Good riddance." As she continued to reach in the back of the drawer, she felt her feet stepping on something gritty under the desk.

She got up from the chair and scooped down to see what it was. It was the pictures and frames she had on her desk to portray she was a happily married woman with a man she had Photo shopped standing next to her. She grabbed all the pictures carefully to not cut her hand on the shattered glass. When she looked at one of the pictures, the word, *fraud*, was written on her face. It was written on every photo. She thought to herself, *Did Jeremiah do this?*

# CHAPTER TWENTY-THREE

Vivian had made it home in time to prepare a meal for her and Jerry. She chose to fix his favorite foods which was spaghetti, fried catfish, and cheesy garlic bread. She was hoping the meal would warm his heart to open up to her about Bianca. She remembered what Evelyn told her about Jerry before she passed away, *the way to her son's heart was through his stomach*. She laughed and almost cried. Even though she only knew Evelyn for a short time she adored her. She saw a fighter in Evelyn and she fought hard until she chose to fight no more. She chose to let God take her home. She saw how strong her faith was and admired Evelyn from the day she met her. Evelyn never showed any weakness or negativity. She may have done it privately, but not once did she show it in front of her family.

Vivian was still confused about why Jerry didn't want to talk to her about Bianca, especially now that she knew Bianca was his sister. Vivian had so many questions she wanted answers and she wanted them today. Not tomorrow or any other day when Jerry got ready to talk.

"Why was he being so secretive about his own sister? Why won't he talk to me? Doesn't he know, there is nothing he could ever do to make me stop loving him? Why won't he talk to me, Lord? I'm his wife. I'm not a stranger in the streets." Vivian asked out loud.

Vivian continued talking to God, "Lord, I remember it like yesterday, the first day we met. He bumped into me by accident with a plate of food in his hands. I wonder if he did that on purpose."

Vivian and Jerry met when they were attending a school function for all the educators in their school district. At that time, Vivian was a Math teacher at a middle school where Jerry was working as a Physical Education teacher. She didn't know he worked there. She wasn't looking for a man at that time. Even if she had seen him, she wouldn't have given him the time of day. Her divorce was finalized two years ago and she was working on herself and her relationship with Jesus Christ. She had given her life to Christ when she was going through with her ex-husband whom she didn't call by name. When she was talking to people or people ask her about him, she referred to him as 'the ex-husband.' At first, she was calling him that to be resentful, but later after being healed from the hurt, she called him by his name. And very seldom did she have to talk about him because she forgave him for the emotional and verbal abuse. Her ex-husband never laid a hand on her, but his words and actions toward her could cut her throat. Not literally, but it came close because Vivian felt like the man was killing her slowly, but surely. Then, one day, she had enough. She couldn't take it anymore. It was never her intention to get married one day and divorced six years later. She wanted her marriage and worked hard to make it work. But at times, it felt like Vivian was alone in making the marriage work. That man never changed.

Not long after Vivian and Jerry started dating, she was promoted to an Assistant Principal position at another school. After three months of dating, Jerry proposed to Vivian and they were married three months after that. Jerry wanted his mother, Evelyn, to be able to attend the wedding. They were told by three different doctors she didn't have long and there was nothing they could do for her. Vivian was hesitant to marry so quickly, but after fasting and praying, she had her answer that Jerry was her husband. She even waited for God to send three confirmations through people at her previous church along with visions and dreams. She was serious about this. She was not going to walk down that aisle until she heard from God herself.

Jerry walked in the house as Vivian was turning the oven off. The aroma of the cheesy garlic bread was thickened through the atmosphere of the house.

"Now, that's what I'm talking about. Something smells good up in here!" Jerry said.

"I hope you're hungry, babe."

"I am famished." Jerry said and walked up to her and kissed her on the lips.

Vivian was glad Jerry was in a good mood. Maybe she would get the answers to her questions about Bianca.

"I see you have cooked my favorites." Jerry said while breaking off a piece of the catfish.

Vivian popped his hand gently.

"Did you wash your hands, babe."

"Oh, my bad."

Jerry washed his hands and went to the table that was already set with plates, silverware, and sweet tea. Vivian joined him at the table with the food. They blessed the food and Jerry dived into the dishes on the table.

"Viv, you will never guess who showed up at my job when I was leaving football practice."

"Who?"

"Joe and some of the Elders from the church. One of the Elders wanted to fight."

"Are you serious?"

"Some young dude. I don't know why Pastor Jones appointed him as an Elder."

"Wow. What did they want?" Vivian said.

"They wanted to know why I told their business." Jerry said before he took a bite of his catfish.

"What did you tell them?"

"I told them they shouldn't have done it."

"What?" Vivian said almost choking on her sweet tea.

"Yeah, I told them they shouldn't have done the things they did. They were talking about their wives weren't talking to them. That's not my fault."

Vivian was appalled that Jerry was telling her all this because lately they hadn't said more than two or three sentences to each other. But she couldn't believe what her ears were hearing. She wanted to scold him, but seeing he was in a good mood changed her mind. Vivian was on a mission for something else greater than this.

"How did they take it?"

"They were upset. They didn't like what I said."

"I can imagine."

"What do you mean?" Jerry said.

Just when Vivian was about to respond, the doorbell rang.

"Are you expecting someone?" Jerry asked.

The doorbell rang again and this time it was continuously.

"No." Vivian asked puzzled.

"I'll get it." Jerry said with agitation.

Jerry answered the door and Bianca pushed her way through the doorway leaving Jerry still standing at the door.

"I didn't say you could come in." Jerry said while closing the front door.

"Forget all that. I want to know why you vandalized my office?" Bianca said.

Vivian got up from the table and walked into the foyer where Bianca and Jerry were standing.

"What are you talking about?" Jerry asked.

"You came to my office and trashed it! I have evidence!" Bianca yelled.

"What evidence?" Jerry asked.

Vivian stood beside Jerry and watched Bianca take a photo out of her purse.

"This?" Bianca said while showing it in Jerry's face.

"What am I supposed to be looking at?"

"Look, you wrote the word, fraud, on my face."

"Are you out of your mind? How would I get into your office? I don't have a key. Woman, you crazy just like your mama." Jerry said and walked off.

"Don't talk about my mama like you know her." Bianca said.

"Who don't know her?" Jerry asked.

"Jerry! That's not a nice thing to say." Vivian said.

"Oh, well, if the shoe fits. I'm going to bed." Jerry said.

"I don't know who this person is, but I want my husband back." Vivian declared.

"I'm here. I haven't gone anywhere." Jerry said as he continued walking upstairs to go to bed.

"The devil is a lie! This is not who God created you to be!" Vivian said aloud so he could hear.

"I'm so sorry, Bianca, on behalf of my husband."

"I don't know how much more I can take." Bianca said in tears.

"Come, have a seat." Vivian said grabbing her hand.

They walked into the living room and sat on the sofa. Vivian passed a box of tissue to Bianca. She grabbed a couple out of the box. She blew her nose and dried her tears off her face.

"What do you mean you don't know how much more you can take?" Vivian asked.

"I feel like I'm under attack. My house was vandalized. A man I had met was not who he claimed to be."

"Wait a minute, I thought you were married."

"That was a lie. I did that to get married clients to trust me. What married woman would talk to a sex therapist who was single?"

"I would."

"Girl, stop lying."

"I'm not lying."

"Well, I would have had only one client."

Bianca and Vivian laughed.

"You know Jerry didn't do this. He was at work all day."

"I know." Bianca sighed.

"Do you have an idea of who is doing this to you?" Vivian asked.

"I'm not one hundred percent sure, but I do have an idea of who it may be. I think it's Yvonne, but I don't want to believe it."

"Who is she to you?" Vivian asked.

"A stalker. For real though, she is a widow. I was dating her husband for three years and didn't know it."

"Are you saying you didn't know he was married?" Vivian asked.

"Yes, that is what I'm saying.?

"How could you not have known?"

"I don't know. He was good at lying. He looked me straight in the eye and told me he wasn't married. I feel so stupid."

"You are not stupid. If you didn't know, you didn't know. And if you did, you would have ended the relationship, right?"

"I don't know if I would have, Vivian."

There was a silence.

"Three years is a long time and you didn't see a sign or something."

"Maybe I didn't want to see." Bianca said.

"Wait a minute, did you say Yvonne was a widow?"

"Yes."

"So, he is dead. Was he with you or with her?"

"You sure do ask a lot of questions?"

"Girl, I can't help it. Jerry don't like it either. He says he feels like he is being interrogated at a police station."

"Exactly."

"I know you're not talking, Dr. Overton."

Bianca smiled.

"You are a doctor, right?"

"Yes, I do have my doctorate."

"See, you're not stupid. *You are smart. You are kind.*" Vivian said.

"*And you are important.*" Bianca and Vivian said simultaneously.

"*The Help* was a good movie." Vivian said.

"Yes, it was, and funny." Bianca said.

"May I ask? What made you go into life coaching and sex therapy? You have a Master's degree in Marriage & Family Therapy."

"Sex is where the money is." Bianca said. "I better go. Thank you." Bianca said.

"For what?" Vivian asked.

"For not judging me."

"Girl, I have no right to judge anyone. You probably wouldn't be my friend, if you knew some of the stuff I used to do."

"Girl, please, you don't look like it."

"Praise Jesus! I don't look like what I've been through. I thank the Lord for Jesus. If anyone is in Christ, they are a new creation and old things pass away and all things are made new."

"I wish I could be made new." Bianca said.

"Do you know Jesus?" Vivian asked.

"Of course, I know Him." Bianca said.

"I mean, do you have a personal relationship with Him. Billy Graham said it best, *religion without a personal encounter with Jesus Christ will not save the soul or bring the peace that your soul longs for.*"

"I like that."

"It's true. I was lost until I had a personal encounter with Christ and I am so glad I gave my life to Him. I was so broken and hurt. He came into my life and mended every brokenness in me and made me whole."

Bianca saw the joy Vivian was expressing when she was talking about her experience with Christ. She longed to feel that way. She wanted to be happy and whole.

"Wow, the look on your face when you're talking."

"What do you mean?"

"You look happy."

"It's joy. Unspeakable joy. No matter what goes on in my life, nobody or anything can take it from me."

"I want that."

"You can have it. Do you accept Jesus as your personal Lord and Savior?

Bianca was about to answer, but her phone vibrated. She took her phone out of her pocket and saw it was an unknown caller. She declined the call and put it back in the pocket. The phone vibrated again. She took the phone out of her pocket and she recognized her landline number on the screen. She answered, "Hello."

"I knew you would answer this time."

"Who is this and how are you calling from my house?" Bianca asked as she stood up from the couch.

"You don't recognize my voice? You sure are dumb and let's not forget, a whoremonger."

"I am not a whoremonger, Yvonne."

"Well, your actions say otherwise."

"How did you get in my house?" Bianca asked.

"How do you think? I have a set of keys. Thanks to Fabien."

Bianca became furious and disconnected the call. She grabbed her purse and told Vivian she had to go.

"What's going on?"

"I have to go."

"Do you need me to come with you?"

"No. I got this. I will call you later." Bianca said and left.

Vivian was concerned. She did what she always did when she didn't know what to do. She prayed for Bianca's safety and guidance for Jerry.

# CHAPTER TWENTY-FOUR

After Vivian had finished praying, she went into the kitchen to clean it. She put the food in Tupperware containers to save for the next day. She was dreading to go upstairs and see Jerry. She was not in the mood to argue with him. Vivian couldn't function when her house didn't feel peaceful. She grew up in a house where it was always chaotic. Her parents argued violently and they would command her to go to her room and put on her music. And that's what Vivian did. She would go in her room, turn on the music, hide in her closet and rock herself to sleep. But her music didn't help. She could still hear them arguing and fighting. Vivian's mother, Sherrie, didn't take any licks from her father without giving it back. She was a short woman, five feet and one inch and her dad was six feet tall. Every time they fought, Vivian always heard her mother say, *don't let my height fool you, I will knock you* out. Thirty minutes later, she would hear the bed squeaking, headboard rhythmically hitting against the wall, and moaning from their bedroom. When Vivian became a teenager, the fights and arguments had ceased. She didn't know what happened to her parents and didn't ask them either. She was glad they weren't fighting anymore.

Vivian failed to realized her parents were the reason for her taking too long to stand up for herself during her first marriage. Her mother always called her timid when she was growing up. Vivian wasn't timid, but she had a passive personality. That was the way she was created by God, but when God gave her a way of escape from her ex-husband, she took it. She drew her strength from the Lord and never looked back. Here she was being the same way with Jerry.

Vivian didn't know what kind of mood Jerry was in and she hoped he was deeply asleep. She took her time cleaning the kitchen. She even mopped the floors, dusted the living room, cleaned the half bathroom, washed a load of towels, folded them, and put them in the closet where they belonged. She tried to find something else to do to avoid going upstairs. She wished she was still a teacher because she could be grading papers. When she realized there was nothing else to clean downstairs. She went upstairs and cleaned the bathroom in the guest room. She vacuumed the carpet in the guest room. After she was done, she walked into their bedroom. Jerry was in the bed snoring.

"Thank God, he's asleep. Lord, I know we need to talk, but I really don't feel like arguing with that man." Vivian whispered to herself.

Vivian took her nightwear out of the drawer and went in the bathroom to shower. When she was done, she got in the bed and grabbed her Bible from the nightstand. She read a few scriptures, wrote some notes, and closed her Bible. She placed it back on the nightstand and turned the lamplight off. She pulled the covers over her shoulder and laid on her left side away from Jerry's snoring.

When she was about ten minutes into her sleep, she felt Jerry's hand rubbing her thigh. His hand began to glide under her gown toward her buttocks and Vivian didn't move an inch. His hand stopped there when he realized she had on panties. And they weren't the sexy ones with the opening. These panties were the ones grandmothers wore that almost covered to the top of their waist. Vivian heard him groaned and turned on his other side away from her.

Vivian knew Jerry was disappointed when he realized she had on panties. Vivian didn't like wearing panties to bed. She believed in keeping herself cool and dry at nighttime. She only wore panties to bed when her menstrual cycle was on and Jerry knew that about her. But what Jerry didn't know was it wasn't time for her menstrual cycle. If he had kept up with her days, he would have known that it wasn't time for *Aunt Flo* to be visiting. Vivian was deliberately wearing those panties to keep him at bay. She wasn't in the mood to be intimate with Jerry tonight. At the rate he was going, it might be another month before she gets back in the mood. She did smile to herself though when she realized her mission was accomplished.

# CHAPTER TWENTY-FIVE

Bianca was on her way home to see if Yvonne was inside her house. As she was driving, she thought about what Vivian had said to her. She liked talking to Vivian. She made her feel comfortable and she felt like she could tell Vivian anything. She was glad she had a chance to tell Vivian everything about faking her marital status to get clients and her relationship with Junior. She hoped to build a friendship with Vivian because she felt like they were kindred sisters. She also believed Vivian could be a good influence. Technically, they were family. Jerry may not want to be in her life, but he couldn't stop Vivian from being in her life. She had been longing to have a friend for a while now. She didn't care if it was one friend or two. All she needed was one and the right one to help her get her life together.

Bianca had made it to her house. She noticed Yvonne's vehicle in her driveway. She parked behind it, got out of her car, and opened the front door of her house which was unlocked.

Yvonne was sitting on the loveseat in the living room with her legs crossed while buffing her fingernails.

"How did you get in here?" Bianca asked.

"I told you. Fabien."

Bianca sighed hard and said, "I don't have time for this foolishness. I'm calling the police."

"Put the phone down." Yvonne said with a .22 gun pointing at Bianca.

Bianca didn't notice it because she was busy looking for the phone in her purse. When she found her phone, she dialed Vivian's cell phone.

Yvonne spoke louder, "I said put the phone down!"

Bianca looked at her with the phone to her ear. She could hear Vivian saying, "Hello."

Bianca pretended like she was disconnecting the call and placed the phone back in her purse. She hoped Vivian was listening and called the police.

"Throw that purse on the couch." Yvonne said.

"Please don't shoot me." Bianca said aloud.

"I'm not going to shoot you... yet." Yvonne said smiling. "We are going to have a talk first."

Bianca moved slowly to the couch.

"No. Come sit beside me over here.

Bianca moved cautiously to the sofa where Yvonne sat down with the gun still pointed at her.

"Have a seat. Don't be afraid. I won't bite."

"It's hard to not be afraid when a gun is pointing at me." Bianca said.

"I would like to know how you met my husband and I want full details."

"We met a gas station. We were next to each other pumping gas in our cars. I left the pump unattended to purchase a bag of chips at the checkout window. The pump inside my car malfunctioned and gas over-flowed. Junior caught it and placed the pump in its dispenser. I thanked him for catching it in time."

"And what else?"

"What do you mean?"

"Did you ask him for his phone number?"

"No. He asked me for mine."

"Stop lying."

"I'm not lying. He asked me for my number and he is the one who called me. I didn't initiate our relation-ship."

"You are a lying whoremonger. Do your mama know you are a homewrecker?"

"Don't talk about my mother like you know her." Bianca stood up from the couch. She couldn't stand when other people talked about her mother, Bonnie. She may not have a close relationship with her Bonnie, but she will always defend her until the day she left this earth.

"I see I hit a nerve." Yvonne smiled.

"I'm not going to sit here and take this crap from you. I'm sorry I was with Junior all these years, but I did not know he was married. If I had known, I would have not entertained that lying piece of..."

"Don't you dare say it?"

"I see I hit a nerve. Don't dish it if you can't take it." Bianca said.

Yvonne raised her gun up at Bianca and screamed, "You, whoremonger, I'm going to kill you."

Bianca ducked down when Yvonne fired that first shot and she missed.

Bianca took off running and Yvonne pulled the trigger again. This time she didn't miss her.

# CHAPTER TWENTY-SIX

When Vivian had answered the phone call from Bianca, she was sleepy. She knew it was Bianca who had called because she had saved her number in her contacts. She heard Bianca mentioned something about don't shoot her. She woke Jerry up so he could listen to the conversation, too. He was groggy, but when he heard Yvonne mentioned not shooting her yet, he grabbed his cell phone to call 911. While they were listening on their phones, they were getting dressed. Jerry gave the dispatcher Bianca's address and disconnected the call. They continued to listen to the conversation between Yvonne and Bianca while they were driving to Bianca's house.

Vivian wondered how Jerry knew where Bianca lived, but she didn't ask him. She chose to focus on

Bianca for the time being because she heard the gun-shots. She prayed God had covered her.

When Vivian and Jerry arrived at Bianca's house, the ambulance and police were there. Vivian saw an officer escorting an older woman to the police car in handcuffs. She saw the paramedics with the stretcher walking to the ambulance. Vivian ran to the stretcher and called Bianca's name. She was stopped by one of the officers before she could make it to Bianca's side.

Bianca heard her name being called and she turned toward the familiar voice. She saw Vivian being stopped by a police officer. She wanted to reach out to her, but she was in excruciating pain. She heard one of the paramedics tell her to relax and that they were going to take care of her.

The paramedics rushed Bianca to the nearest hospital. When they arrived at the hospital and took her out of the ambulance, she recognized the familiar voice and opened her eyes. It was Dr. Holden as her attending doctor. She thought to herself, *Lord, not this crazy one*.

Jerry and Vivian were at the hospital in the waiting room. Jerry had mixed feelings. He didn't like Bianca, but he didn't want her to die. Vivian was sitting next to him and she saw him wiping his eyes. She was still mad at him, but she wasn't too mad to minister to him. She grabbed his hand and told him everything would be alright. She believed God wasn't through with Bianca yet.

"We should pray." Vivian said.

"You're right." Jerry said.

They stood up from their seats and held hands. They didn't care there was another couple in the waiting room because they may need prayer, too. When Vivian was about to pray, Jerry intercepted.

"Our Father, who is in heaven. Hallowed be thy name. Let thy kingdom come and thy will be done. I pray Father God that you will forgive me for what I have done. I have not made good decisions concerning your people and my wife, Viv. The wife you have given me to love and cherish. I need your strength to do better and I hope to have another chance to amend my relationship with her and the members at my church. Please open their hearts to forgive me for I have sinned. God, I don't want to be this person anymore. I don't like who I have become. Renew me, Lord, Restore me back to your good grace. Please don't let my shortcomings stop us from coming boldly to your throne Lord God for we need you. We need you now. We can't do anything without you, Lord. Your word says if we ask, it shall be given We are here to ask in the name of Jesus that You be in the surgery room on behalf of Bianca. She is fighting for her life and we believe through the blood of Jesus that she will live and not die. We are asking for you to give Bianca another chance to see your glory. Another chance to walk out of here knowing who you are and who she belongs to. We are also praying for this couple in the room. We pray you meet their need. Release your comfort and peace. A peace that surpasses all understanding. May they walk out of here in victory and not with their heads down, Lord. You are able to do anything. There is absolutely nothing too hard for you, God. Many are the afflictions of the righteous, but you, God will deliver us out of them all. We pray this prayer in the name of Jesus. Amen."

"Amen." Vivian said.

The woman who was sitting down was on her feet in tears praising God. Her husband was still sitting down with tears in his eyes. Vivian and Jerry didn't know what they were going through, but they could tell they needed a breakthrough. The woman's husband walked toward Jerry and shook his hand. He gave him thanks for praying. He mentioned he and his wife needed to be reminded of who God was. Vivian was at the woman's side providing her with tissue.

Dr. Holden walked into the waiting room.

"Is everything alright."

The woman who was standing near Vivian said, "Yes. All is well."

"How is she, doctor?"

"Oh, yes, Bianca is in stable condition. It was a blessing that the bullet didn't hit any major organs. It was two inches away from her heart."

"Praise God!" Vivian said.

"Thank you, Jesus!" Jerry said.

"Can we see her, doctor?

"She is out of recovery. She should be in a room in 15 minutes."

"Thank you, doctor." Jerry said.

"Sure, no problem. You all have a good night."

Fifteen minutes had passed. Jerry and Vivian were sitting near Bianca's bed. They were waiting for her to wake up. Ten more minutes passed and Bianca was slowly waking up.

"Bianca." Vivian said quickly getting out of her seat.

"Vivian, is that you?"

"Yes. Jerry and I are here."

"Jerry, too?"

"Yes. I'm here." Jerry said.

"I am so glad to see you both here and thank you for calling the police."

"Girl, of course, we weren't going to let anything happen to you." Vivian said.

"We were praying for you."

"Both of you prayed for me?" Bianca said with her voice cracking.

"God is not through with you yet." Vivian declared.

"When that woman shot me, it sure felt like it was over."

"Nope, it is not over." Vivian said.

Bianca covered her eyes to hide her tears.

"It's okay. Let it out. Tears are meant to be shed, not hidden, especially in a situation like this." Vivian said while handing tissue to Bianca.

"Thank you." Bianca said while accepting the tissue.

Jerry was quiet in his seat.

"Vivian, would you let me talk to Jerry alone. I need to tell him something."

Vivian hesitated and looked at Jerry. He didn't say anything, but he did stand up. Vivian said, "Sure," and walked out of the room wondering what they had to talk about that couldn't be said in front of her.

"Jerry, I want you to know, what happened between us was not your fault. It was our dad's fault. This is on him, not us. You have no reason to be shame and feeling guilty. I have made my peace with it and forgive you. It is time for you to forgive yourself. I want you and Vivian to be my family and this hate you have for me is tearing me apart."

"I don't hate you."

"Okay, then, prove it. Tell Vivian about us tonight. Not tomorrow or any other day. Tell her tonight."

"Okay."

"Promise me, Jeremiah."

"I promise I will tell her tonight. Get some rest. We will be back to see you tomorrow, sis."

Bianca smiled and cried again.

"Don't cry."

"I can't help it. These are tears of joy."

"Alright, we will see you tomorrow."

After Jerry left Bianca's room. She gave praise to God for saving her. She remembered the conversation she had with Vivian. She raised her arms up high and said, "Jesus, I accept you as my personal Lord and Savior. I confess with my mouth that you are Lord, the one who died for me and my sins. I want to be made new, Jesus. I want to be whole! Create in me a clean heart and renew a right spirit within me. I'm ready to have a personal encounter with you."

Jerry and Vivian had arrived home. It was after midnight and Vivian was tired.

"I'm going to bed."

"Viv, I need to tell you something."

"What is it, Jerry? You're scaring me."

"That's not my intention. Have a seat. I have to get this off my chest." Jerry said as he sat next to her.

"Okay." Vivian said and sat down.

"A long time ago, actually ten years ago, Bianca and I were dating. We didn't know we were kin to each other until Bianca introduced me to her mother. I remember it like yesterday. She kept asking us did we sleep together. We never did give her an answer. We were trying to figure out why she was being so dramatic. She finally told us we had the same daddy. Immediately, I got mad. The more she kept asking us if we slept with each other, the madder I got. I left Bianca and her mother screaming at each other and never looked back. I wiped the whole ordeal from my mind and disowned her. I didn't want to have any-thing do with Bianca. I even cursed our dad's grave."

"Why?"

"Because I was ashamed."

"But, babe, you didn't know. You didn't know your dad had another child with another woman. You are not responsible for your father's sins. Lay down that heavy weight and forgive yourself and your dad."

"I will, with the Lord's help. I will."

"Thank you for telling me. That couldn't have been easy." Vivian said and gave Jerry a passionate kiss. She knew how much he loved her kisses. And it didn't stop there, they ended on the stairs. They had an intense make up session on the stairs that made Vivian's toes curls and fists clinched. At last, her thirst for Jerry was quenched. She was on cloud nine and didn't want it to end.

# CHAPTER TWENTY-SEVEN

A week had pass. Vivian and Jerry arrived at the church to attend Marriage Ministry. They were both elated with joy that Bianca was finally at home recovering and wanted to give God praise in the house of God. They didn't care that people were looking at them. Their focus was on the Lord and not them. Jerry had a lot to be thankful for and he wasn't going to let their beady eyes distract him from giving God the praise that was due onto Him.

Vivian had called Pastor Jones and asked him if she could say a few words during the meeting. It was much needed to restore the couples in the Marriage Ministry. Pastor Jones was hesitant at first, but he agreed to let her speak. Vivian promised him it was going to be nothing but the Word of God flowing through the meeting. She was not going to speak discord and confusion because God do not cause confusion.

When the praise team was done singing, Vivian became fearful. She went to the bathroom and stood in the mirror. She quoted her favorite scripture, "Lord, you did not give me the spirit of fear. You have given me love, power, and a sound mind. I rebuke fear right now in the name of Jesus."

Vivian walked inside the room where the Marriage Ministry was located. She could tell people were waiting on her. Jerry jumped from his seat to assist her at the podium. When she was situated, Jerry sat down in his seat in front of her.

"Good evening, everyone!" Vivian said.

"Good evening."

"First, I want to thank Pastor Jones and First Lady for giving me the opportunity to speak tonight. I had no intention to do something like this, but I have to be obedient to God. Before I get into the lesson, my husband, Jerry would like to say something."

Vivian heard the couples groaned and Pastor Jones was shaking his head in disappointment at Vivian.

"I know he is the last person you want to hear from, but before you make your minds up about him, please give him a chance to speak."

Vivian moved to the side when Jerry joined her at the podium.

"All I want to do is come up here and apologize for my behavior. It was not my right to share your business. I was wrong. I was also wrong for putting the spotlight on you guys to keep you from looking at me. I have had a long hard look at myself and I didn't like what I saw. To be honest, I haven't liked what I saw for a long time. I was feeling abandoned by my biological dad who, by the way, was the one who taught me about pornography. It was his way of bonding with a twelve-year-old. He told me his dad watch porn with him when he was teenager and he was passing it on to me. After he had passed, I guess I continued to watch porn convincing myself it was the only way to be close to him. Yeah, I know how twisted that sounds, but to a teenager who never knew his dad to the fullest, it wasn't. I know I'm not perfect, but I am a work in progress. Would you all please forgive me? I didn't mean to jeopardize your marriages. I am so sorry, Pastor Jones and First Lady, Deborah. I had no right digging in your past, especially after all you have done for me Pastor Jones. You have been my mentor and you took me under your wing when I was in college. Will you forgive me?"

The couples looked at Pastor Jones to see his next move. He ascended from his chair and walked toward Jerry.

"Peter asked Jesus, how many times should I forgive my brother who sinned against me, is it seven times? Jesus told Peter it was seventy times seven. So, yes, Jeremiah, I forgive you. I was disappointed in you, but I forgive you."

Pastor Jones hugged Jerry. The rest of the couples walked toward Jerry to tell him they forgive him, too, including the young Elder who wanted to fight him.

# CHAPTER TWENTY-EIGHT

Bianca decided to visit Yvonne in jail. She was indicted for attempted murder. She was in jail waiting for a trial date to be set. She didn't have anyone to bail her out. Junior was dead, her mother was in the nursing home, and she wasn't on speaking terms with her only sibling. Bianca was going through the metal detectors. She didn't know she had to go through so much trouble to visit somebody in jail. They were serious about safety. They took her phone. If she knew they were going to do that, she would have locked it up in the glove compartment in her car. She was getting a little paranoid at some of the stares she was getting from the other people who were in the visitation room. They were looking impatient and tired. Bianca almost decided to turn around and get back in her car. She wasn't feeling comfortable. She wished she had taken Vivian's offer to accompanied her to the jailhouse. She had talked to her that morning letting her know she was getting cold feet. Vivian assured her that she was doing the right thing.

Yvonne came into the visitation room and she saw Bianca waving for her. She walked toward Bianca's table smiling.

"Well, look who came to visit me? The whoremonger."

"I would appreciate it if you would stop calling me that because that is not who I am. I am in Christ Jesus and I am no longer condemned by my past."

"Is that so?"

"Yes. It is so." Bianca said with confidence.

"You know, when they told me I had a visitor. I didn't expect it to be you."

"Well, it's me."

"What do you want?"

"I came here to tell you I forgive you."

Yvonne laughed loudly and Bianca looked at her. She couldn't figure out what was funny.

"You forgive me? Woman, you should be asking me for forgiveness."

"How do you figure that?" Bianca said.

"You were sleeping with my husband!" Yvonne yelled so the other visitors in the room could hear.

"I didn't know he was your husband. How long are you going to hold this grudge against me?"

"For as long as I can, until hell freezes over, and I guess, that will be never." Yvonne chuckled.

"Why are you so bitter?"

"Baby, you don't have enough time in the world to hear my story."

"Well, give me the short version."

"I don't think so. I don't know you." Yvonne said.

"You're right, you don't know me, but I want to know you."

"Girl, please don't show me no pity."

"I'm not."

"Yes, you are. I have no regrets for anything I have done in my life."

"Are you saying you don't regret putting yourself in jail?"

"No. Shooting you in the back was the highlight of my life."

"I feel sorry for you." Bianca said.

"Didn't I just tell you I didn't want your pity."

"I didn't mean like that."

"You don't mean a lot of things. I bet you are a daddy's girl. He spoiled you rotten and there was nothing lacking in your life. He made sure you had all you needed to be a successful black woman, but here you are begging me to forgive you."

"I wasn't begging you. I came here to let you know I forgave you for shooting me in the back. That was very low."

"I know."

"I could have died."

"That was my intention."

"I don't know why I came here."

"I don't know why you came here, either. There's the door if you want to leave."

"I might as well because this conversation is not productive. Bye, Yvonne. Again, I apologize for the hurt I may have caused you."

Bianca walked away from the table. She wasn't sure if she put a dent in Yvonne's heart, but that was not her concern. It was in God's hands. She did what she was told to do and that was to plant a seed and God will take care of the rest. Bianca got her things and got in her car to leave. She was no longer feeling burdened by what Yvonne did to her. She had laid it aside and given it to God. She let down the window on the driver's side to feel the breeze.

"No more bondage. I am free and free indeed." Bianca said.

# EPILOGUE

Four months had passed since Bianca visited Yvonne in jail. She was at the church in one of the rooms with Vivian getting prepared to be baptized. Her life had never been the same since she had accepted Christ as her Lord and Savior. She finally knew what Vivian was talking about when she was sharing her experience of Christ. Bianca felt free, loved, and happy. Now she was sealing her faith, so she said, with baptism. She wished her grandmother, Beatrice, was alive to see how far she had come. She did invite Bonnie to come see her be baptized. She even took her shopping for a new dress and they got their nails and hair done together. Bonnie had not seen Bianca smile this much since her husband, Victor had passed. She may not have had a close relationship with Bianca, but it was always her desire for her daughter to be happy. Bonnie was ushered to sit on the front row at the request of Bianca. Bonnie had never felt so welcome, loved, and warmth in a church before. At first, she thought she would be judged until so many women approached to greet her. They didn't shake her hand, they gave her warm hugs. She felt overwhelmed and almost wanted to cry. She thought to herself, "God, if you keep this up, I just might join this church."

In Bianca's case, she did join, two months ago and had been coming faithfully ever since. She was teaching Sunday School to a group of four-year-old children and she loved it. She was also singing in the choir every Sunday. When she wasn't singing, she was a greeter at the front door. Vivian teased her about her activity in the church.

"Is there anything you're not going to do in this church?"

"Girl, I'm on the run for Christ. Whatever he tells me to do, that's what I'm going to do."

Vivian laughed and said, "Such a baby in Christ."

"What is that supposed to mean?"

"Right now, you're on the run for Christ, but wait until the real work begins, that is within you."

"I don't understand."

"You will. Keep living." Vivian said.

"I am." Bianca said with confidence.

"That you are, that you are, my sister. You are living and not just existing. You are living with a purpose." Vivian said.

"What's wrong? Are you okay?"

"I don't know. I feel nauseous."

"Well, let's go to the bathroom. Come on, I will go with you."

Bianca escorted Vivian to the bathroom, but when they got to the hallway, Vivian took off running holding her mouth. Bianca gave Vivian a disgusted look.

"Go ahead, girl. I'm right behind you."

Bianca stood there watching Vivian run to the bathroom and put her hands on her hips.

"Lord, I hope she doesn't have the stomach virus. That is the last thing I need right now."

"Hello, Bianca."

Bianca turned to the voice of a man who called her name. He was standing behind her to the side.

"Hello." Bianca said and looked at the man closer. "Do I know you?"

"You know of me."

"You look familiar, but I don't think so." Bianca said and walked away.

"I'm Fabien."

Bianca stopped in her tracks, lifted her head to the ceiling, and said, "Now, that's a name I do know and wish I hadn't."

Bianca continued walking on toward the bathroom

Fabien spoke a little louder, "Bianca, please hear me out."

"What is it that you have to say? I'm good. I don't need anything from you, not an empty apology. Not your money, if you got any? I don't need a thing from you." Bianca said while facing him.

Fabien walked toward her, and Bianca crossed her arms.

"I didn't come here for you, I came here for… No, I didn't say that right."

Fabien took a deep breath. Bianca stood there nonchalant like she didn't have a care in the world.

"I came to give you a sincere apology. What I did was foul, and it wasn't called for. I was at my lowest point and desperate for money. I did what I did to get money from that woman."

Bianca dropped her arms and looked at Fabien with compassion.

"Thank you for the apology and owning up to your actions." Bianca said.

"I do take responsibility for the hurt I have caused you, Bianca. You didn't deserve any of it, no matter what that woman said. I don't even know her name."

"Yvonne is her name." Bianca said.

"You look like you're not mad at her."

"I'm not. I forgave her. And I forgive you, too, Fabien."

"Thank you. How's business going?"

"It's going great, actually. It was an experience telling my clients the truth about my relationship status. Something I have lied about to get clients for money. I lost quite a bit of clientele, but God has restored my business. The truth was not as bad as I thought."

"It shall make you free."

"Exactly." Bianca said.

"There's something I need to share with you."

"Okay." Bianca said looking at Fabien with her undivided attention.

"That day when you saw me on the corner. I ran from you like a coward, and I was. When you were in your car while I was hiding, I heard you. I felt so convicted and disappointed in the man who I had become. I didn't belong in the streets. I chose to be on the streets. I had my reasons and I became a victim. I didn't want to be victorious. I wanted my family back. My wife, Ryan, and my daughter, Aubree. I haven't said their names in years." Fabien sniffled.

"That's a good thing. You're being healed."

"That's a good way to put it. When I ran from you after you had prayed and stuff. As I was running across the street, I remember, thinking to myself, I hope she prays for me."

Bianca wiped tears from her eyes.

"And I did. As mad as I was at you, I prayed. I saw a need and not an enemy." Bianca said.

"And I want to thank you for that because I was in need."

"And thank you for telling me all this. Look at us, crying like babies, snot coming out of our noses."

Vivian was behind Bianca handing her tissue.

"Here you go." Vivian said.

"Girl, you keep everything in that purse." Bianca laughed.

"Yep, that's why it's so heavy. About to break my shoulders down."

"I better go. I don't want to hold you from being baptize." Fabien said.

"Okay. It was nice seeing you again." Bianca said.

Fabien walked away.

"Wait, Fabien, is that your real name?" Bianca asked.

"Believe it or not, it is."

"What's your last name?"

"Bianca, no ma'am." Vivian said.

"I just want to know."

Fabien approached her and said, "Here's my card. It has my last name and my cell number."

"Fabien Davis, it is so nice to meet you." Bianca said while extending her hand toward him.

"It is nice to meet you, too, Bianca Overton." Fabien said and shook her hand.

Fabien walked away and went into the sanctuary of the church.

Vivian was standing there with her arms crossed and shaking her head at Bianca.

"What? There's nothing wrong with conversation. You remember when I said watch out for the hard work that is within you."

"Yeah, what does that have to do with this?"

"Paul said it best, if anyone want to follow Jesus, they must deny themselves and take up his cross daily."

"That's not exactly how it is written in the Bible."

"Well, I'm just paraphrasing. I didn't take away or add anything to the Word. Now, give me this here."

"Excuse me, can I have my card back."

"Yep, when you start eating meat, I will give it back."

"What does meat have to do with this? I see I have a lot to learn."

Vivian and Bianca walked into the room where they were getting prepared for the baptism.

"Are you feeling better? I hope you don't have a stomach virus.".

"It's not a stomach virus." Vivian said and started to cry.

"What 's wrong?"

Vivian wiped her tears with tissue and said nothing.

"Vivian, what is the matter?"

"I think I'm pregnant."

"Really, that's good news. I'm going to be an auntie." Bianca said.

Vivian sighed.

"Why you're not happy? This is not good news for you?"

"It is, but…"

"But what?"

"It's bad timing."

"How so?"

"This is between me and you." Vivian said.

"Of course." Bianca said with concern.

"Jerry lost his job. He was terminated."

"No. Why?"

"He is being accused of allowing some students to look at pornographic magazines at school. Jerry said he didn't bring any of those magazines to the school."

"Do you believe him?"

"To be honest, Bianca, I don't." Vivian said quietly.

TO BE CONTINUED

Thank you for reading my book! If you enjoyed it, please take a moment and leave me a review.

# Acknowledgments

Gratefulness is how I feel right now as I write this acknowledgment. I am **grateful to God** for showing me I had more inside of me than I could ever imagine. His word rings true, *eyes haven't seen, ears haven't heard, and neither have entered the heart of man, the things which God has prepared for them who love him*. Through the strength of Jesus, I have written this novel and all glory belongs to the **King of Glory**.

I want to thank my husband, friend, lover, and prayer partner, **Jeffrey Rowell**. I love you and thank you for believing in me more than I believed in myself. I want to thank my mother, **Margaret Terry,** and **siblings** for their love and support and always being my number one fans. I want to thank my kindred sister, **Karolyn Taylor**, for always keeping me focus when I doubt who I am in God.

I also want to **thank all of my readers in advance** for supporting my first (teaser) novel. I pray you visit my website and follow me. I am not done writing and there is so much to talk about in this novel. There are discussion questions available for book clubs and ministries.

## ABOUT THE AUTHOR

Tyra E. Rowell, a Counselor by day and an Author by night. This is her first Christian Fiction novel. She has also written a non-fiction book, *Unapologetically Being Me*.

It has always been Tyra's dream to be a novelist from the time she graduated high school. It took many years for her to see this dream to fruition, but Tyra believes everything is on God's timing.

She is a loving mother, devoted wife, and an innovative woman with a gift of teaching who has Jesus as the center of her life.

Check out her website and Facebook page to stay updated on her upcoming novel which is a sequel.

www.tyrarowell.com
www.facebook.com/tyraerowell

## Group Discussion Questions

1.  Do you think Vivian's desperate plea for help with her sex life is more common among married women of faith?

2.  Do you think Jerry's addiction to pornography is his fault for not being able to please Vivian? Do you think he should have been taking notes from watching pornography?

3.  Why was Vivian afraid to communicate with Jerry that she was unhappy with their sex life?

4.  Do you think Vivian's past sexual experiences had an influence on her intimacy in the bedroom?

5.  Do you think the husband have any idea of how frustrated it is for the wife to be orgasmic deprived or bored from the repetition in the bedroom?

6.  Should the wife expect the husband to do all the work? What's wrong with the wife being dominant in the bedroom?

7.  Do you think Vivian needed Dr. Overton's help? Did she have any impact on Vivian's decisions?

8.  Should Jerry have told the members' secrets during Marriage Ministry? Why do you think he did it in the first place?

9.  What kind of feelings did you have toward First Lady Jones? Why do you think she stayed with her husband after all he had done?

10. Do you think Vivian and Jerry was having sexual issues because they had got married swiftly? Or because they didn't test the water before marriage?

11. Do you think Bianca being a fatherless child had an impact on her unwise decisions with men?

12. Is there something wrong with Bianca wanting to be loved?

13. Do you think it was wrong for Yvonne to be upset with Bianca? Why do you think she went to extreme measures to make Bianca's life miserable? Have you ever wanted to make someone's life miserable?

14. Bianca knew of the Lord, but she didn't have a personal relationship with Jesus Christ. How is that possible? Have you had a personal encounter with Jesus Christ? If yes, how did it feel?

15. Do you think incest among relatives who have no idea they are kin is common? Would you have been able to forget you were intimate with your half-kin like Bianca did? Do you think Jerry had a right to disown Bianca?

16. Name some of the customs of the world women used to get what they need in the bedroom?

17. When Fabien was first introduced in this novel, what did you think of him? What did you think of Dr. Holden?

18. Do you think married and single people could learn from each other?

19. How could Bianca give Vivian such profound advice and her own life was a mess?

20. How do you think Jerry felt when Vivian told him she wasn't happy with their sex life? Do you think all men would feel this way?